Tales from Pine Hill

◆

John Eppolito, M.D.

Writers Club Press
San Jose New York Lincoln Shanghai

Tales from Pine Hill

Writers Club Press
an imprint of iUniverse.com, Inc.

For information address:
iUniverse.com, Inc.
5220 S 16th, Ste. 200
Lincoln, NE 68512
www.iuniverse.com

ISBN: 0-595-15898-6

Printed in the United States of America

All characters are fictional creations inspired by many real life stories and do not represent any single individuals.

Introduction

◆

A morning fog had lifted over the countryside this spring morning as the sun emulated the morning dew on the glittering fields. From the view out of my medical office window at Pine Hill I could see the school buses arriving at the high school. Across the road was a picturesque red dairy barn. The cows had been milked hours ago and now were out to pasture. The highway's traffic seemed to be headed in one direction, to the large urban region of employment 25 miles away. Deer graced the distant fields and woods and the sound of Canadian geese overhead sang a familiar song. It was another day in the life of a country doctor. The waiting room was filling up and it wasn't yet 8:00 a.m. My three nurses looked hurried with one making the comment to get my roller skates on today. I hope not, I was a terrible roller skater. Before the phones and the patients started, I went back to my office with a fresh cup of coffee in hand to look at the view from Pine Hill one more time. As the view outside was one of country splendor, the view inside of my Pine Hill medical office was one more of country flavor.

When I bought the building ten years ago, it had been a restaurant and a popular truck stop until it was converted by the townspeople into a medical office. The builder did a reasonable job with ample waiting room space which often tends to be an unintended social gathering spot for the locals. I often overhear their sharing of ailments and remedies. It's amazing how many different medical opinions there are just in my own waiting room. One drawback was that the builder put the two bathrooms by the waiting area and none in the back of the building for the staff. This would prompt me to often attempt to sneak past the waiting room in hopes I could have a few moments of uninterrupted peace and quiet.

An ambulance and handicap ramp was conveniently built with access directly into our own little emergency treatment room, fairly well-equipped to handle most medical and minor surgical emergencies. It was the room the local volunteer ambulance folks seemed to frequent quite often. Many of the older folks, stubborn as they may be, would often refuse to go to an Emergency Room or call me in the middle of the night because they didn't feel it would be nice to interrupt me. They would often wait and show up at my office with a variety of cardiac and pulmonary symptoms that should not have waited. I often would remind them of that as they would be whisked away in the ambulance.by our local volunteer ambulance crew.

My other four exam rooms have the standard wall-to-wall color posters of all known body organ parts. My staff of three nurses felt I needed a splash of color so I had the old knotty pine paneling painted over to a brighter cream with a green trim and I added a lot of bargain Wal-Mart scenic prints. This place looked a little tacky, but it was home, it was country and it worked. The nice thing about most of the exam rooms were that they had great views of pine woods. This was a great asset to get a good, quick fix of mental relaxation, on sometimes turbulent days.

My staff of three nurses ran my office. Each had their duties and kept things flowing. Sharon work station was always orderly as was the lab she kept. The main office and reception area for which Debbie and Margaret held domain, housed nearly 7,000 to 8,000 active patient charts. This site justified the federally designated position shortage area that it was and that we were called. An orderly chaos existed in this region of medical office. Sometimes, I would wander in there and then realize it would be better to leave to a safer area.

This rural area, which incorporates many townships, has a gentle, rolling hill landscape, dotted with many farms. Wildlife, including deer and geese, are abundant, and many small lakes and wetlands support a diverse habitat.

The four seasons are distinct, with beautiful summers, colorful falls, fragrant springs and, often, harsh winters accented by nearby Lake Ontario's lake-effect snow falls. Winter can begin here in November and last until mid-April, often resulting in hazardous roads and closing the schools.

But overall, there seems to be a consistency here. Things change very slowly, not only in the natural world, but also among the people. "Set in their ways," is more like it.

Country roads are named after farm families: Ferris Road, Bradt Road. Many of the patriarchs and matriarchs of these farms had eight to twelve children. Many of these children, now in their fifties and sixties, married members of other local large families.

So you can see I avoid field days and never make comments outside my office: I have never seen so many cousins in one region. Add in divorce and remarriage, and you now need a score card.

Most people now commute into nearby urban regions for work. What was once a fairly self-sustaining, independent area of farms and small industries and businesses has now succumbed to the late twentieth century pressures and transitions. Many people are skilled blue-collar workers with years of experience in close-by Fortune 500 and smaller industries. Some are close to retirement, and some are feeling the pinch of downsizing. Others new to the area tend to be mid-level managers, teachers, and some professionals looking for a quiet community, 10 acres of land, and a solitude of mind free from the hassles of living in populated areas. There also remains a sizable population of under-educated, unskilled people of all ages, who live in absolute poverty, with very poor living conditions and often very poor health.

Prior to the time I began my practice, the federal government attempted to place a physician here. Ten years and ten physicians brought little success until I arrived, served back my government aid for medical school, and then decided to stay and purchase the medical practice and building from the local community.

Some of the elders of the community were somewhat indoctrinated by an older M.D. who has since retired. He gave a lot of B12 shots and other remedies: I didn't have a clue what they were for. If took many years to break some of the old habits. And some I never changed because it appeared these treatments weren't doing any harm, and it wasn't worth risking losing some folks by having them avoid reasonable preventive health care. Overall, the old doctor was revered, loved, and respected by his patients, and that in and of itself was vitally important in their overall state of health. Being a doctor that cared about their overall well being, I began to realize, was half the battle in keeping them well. The other half was knowledge, and that involved keeping up monthly on the rapidly changing nature of medical treatments.

The majority of rural medical challenges were the same challenges as in every corner of America, be they urban, suburban, or rural. But there are some day-to-day aspects of rural medicine that are unique and could not be taught in conventional medical school. Many of these aspects have to do with the resilient and sometimes stubborn nature of folks in the country.

For many years, we have concentrated on super specialties, which has resulted in treating parts but not the whole person. With an explosion in technology—and medical malpractice suits—you do not have to be a brain surgeon to understand where this specialization has led us economically as a nation. Couple this with an increasing life expectancy, and we are faced with an extraordinary financial stress on all Americans with regard to private insurance premiums, direct medical costs, and taxes to support medicare and medicaid.

Recently, managed care, driven by market demands, has exploded and has been somewhat successful in slowing the inflationary cycle of health care. A large part of the success of managed is due to the incorporation of primary care providers as gatekeepers to individuals into the health care system. This has recently led more graduates of medical schools to choose family medicine.

We still have a long way to go in moving our national health care system to one which emphasizes prevention and health care maintenance as the means to reducing costs. We must begin to realize that we cannot separate the parts from the whole.

Millions of people realize this, as can be witnessed by the explosion of the alternative health and medicine industry.

Medicine, with its many successes in the specialties, has positively transformed modern life. Conventional medicine, though still has its failures and shortsidedness. As a rural family doctor, I would like to share some stories with you , tales of the human spirit,places where I believe medicine needs to go.

Getting there.

I remember the exact date and time I arrived at Pine Hill, but I often wondered how I got there. Having just attended a medical school reunion rekindled some introspective searching. Did I make the right decisions? How did I get to become a family doctor? Could I have been a super-specialist bringing in the big bucks or worked on new medical research to cure diseases yet unconquered? Did I waste the chances when the opportunities arose?

On my usual twenty mile trek to work past numerous farms and a few small villages was when these thoughts and ideas would reign supreme. After seeing scores of patients with a plethora of problems my evening drive home would take me down the west side of Skaneateles lake. Opening my eyes to the view of this beautiful pristine glacier formed lake nestled in the hills reminded me why.

The reality of the matter was that I knew at an early age that I would become a family doctor. My hometown hero was our family doctor, a constant source of inspiration to me.

However, it was not a cakewalk getting into medical school in the seventies. Many college friends and future colleagues can verify this after spending numerous years in Mexican or European medical schools. I was fortunate in that I was accepted stateside and right in my back yard at SUNY Upstate.

The day I was accepted was quite memorable. It was one week prior to the start of the fall semester and I had been sweating out the final word whether I would be in or out. I was glad that my parents found out first. They were jubilant as no one from either my mother's Irish side or my father's Italian side of the family had ever become a physician. My only surviving grandparent was there that day also. She was ninety years old and had immigrated from Sicily as a teenager but still spoke very little English. Her spirit was glowing. I somehow felt this to be a much bigger day for all of them. They had struggled ; saved and encouraged their children to do the best that they were capable of all of their lives. I now realize that I was living the American dream, thanks to the firm foundation they had laid down for me.

Medical school passed quickly. During this period of time was when I first met my soul mate . We would be married six years later after a lot of years of education and training for both of us and a tremendous amount of miles on that poor Toyota pickup truck of mine.

While I was interviewing for a residency training program in my last year of medical school, one mind opening event occurred that clarified some inner feelings. I was interviewing at a program in Connecticut and stayed over with a close friend . Mick was a carpenter by trade. He had seen numerous physicians who referred him onto other specialists for a disorder relating to his back. After thousand of dollars in fees , diagnostic testing and medications he could not find relief of his pain. I just happened to be there the evening he decided to see an alternative healer for advice and treatment. After being in and out of classroom , hospitals, and clinics for the last four years I responded "sure, why not". Mick drove over and laughed about the coincidence of me being there that evening. As we entered Don's little office , a quiet unassuming man appeared. Don went to work with Mick after he introduced himself. Immediately I watched him connect with Mick and his ailment . It was as if he could visualize the areas of discomfort in Micks spine and then laid out a strategy to correct his problem that they would work on together. After their initial session was complete ,Don turned to me and not knowing a thing about me asked ,"Have we met before John." I answered don't know, I don't think so Don". "Feels like we have" Don said and continued" For some reason I have this vision about you. People are coming to see you for help and leaving in a better state of mind and health . There are lots of pine trees , a very pretty country setting and where you live, this beautiful lake with pines and maple trees with a magnificent view. I listened in an enchanted state as Don asked me a question that I had a feeling he had already known. " So John , what is it that you do"?

"I'm in my last year of medical school, Don" I answered.

Don winked back and smiled , replying "Nice coincidence to meet you".

"It was a pleasure" as we shook hands goodbye.

Looking back I now realize that he had visualized my future office and our home on the lake. Neither of these places would become a reality to me for several more years and without any preconceived notion that I had at the time we met. After all the years of formal education and training that event remains with me. It is so important to keep your mind and soul open to the possible.

My residency training years passed ,quickly in Buffalo with one-hundred hour work weeks, ,sleepless nights and emergencyroom moonlighting . The human experience in those years was sometimes over whelming. I often wondered that during those years that I , like so

many other resident physicians , had become desensitized and sometimes detached from those in need. I was hoping that this was a result
of residency burnout . It was on my mind as I walked through the ruins
of Hippocrates home with my wife Michelle on our journey to the
Greek Isles.

Suddenly, I arrived in this little rural town, agreeing to serve at least
four years in order to pay back my medical tuition costs. Upon leaving
for work on that very first day, I recall Michelle's first words of encour-
agement. " Knock em dead" she said. "Knock em dead" I thought.
Visions of malpractice trial lawyers, sympathetic jurors and chapter
eleven suddenly entered my head. We both laughed as she realized,
especially being an intensive care unit nurse , that she could have chosen
a little softer phrase. Oh how vital that perspective sense of humor is.

At the end of my first day as a country doctor I remembered why I
was here. It was simply to make a difference in the lives of these people
and their families. Little did I know what a difference they would all
make in mine.

Time is Money

♦

Early on this bright, brisk, spring morning, George walked into my office with his hand in a bag of ice, his boots covered with cow dung. After examining his hand, I found that he apparently had a boxer fracture of the fifth metacarpal bone of his right hand—a typical fracture after hitting *someone* or *something* with a closed fist. George had just punched one of his cows. He did it to try to keep her in her pen as she was attempting to run free. Unfortunately, he connected, and we both shared a laugh as I set his fracture.

George was a dairy farmer who, like all farmers, was up at 4:30 a.m. and worked until sleep, seven days a week. He went right back to work the same day. He always said to me impatiently that "Time is money" and "Hell, I can't afford to be sitting around in a doctor's office."

George later returned in a month. "How's the hand George?", I asked.

"Good as new Doc. I don't know what got into me that day," replied humbly. "Doc, been real dizzy lately.Can you figure out what the hell is the matter with me ? George continued "How long have you been having dizzy spells?" I asked.

"Long enough that they've been bothering me," he replied.

"Weeks, months?" I continued.

"Oh, awhile, I guess a few months (pause) hell, who knows maybe I've been dizzy all my life," George said.

"Can you describe your dizzy spells, George? Do they last longer than a few seconds or minutes and how often do they last?" I continued.

"Jesus, you ask a lot of questions," George snapped back. Then he thought, "Well, they just come, sometimes, when I'm not doing anything."

"Do you get a sensation of the room spinning or you spinning and is it made worse by any sudden position?" I asked.

"No, not really. Can't say I do Doc," he said. "Sometimes, I get the feeling I can't breath, my hands both go numb and then I feel real light-headed. It happens a lot more lately, Doc."

"Does it happen when you're doing heavy chores or heavy exertional work and do you get any chest pain?", I asked.

"Can't say I do, Doc," George replied. Then he started getting fidgety. "Shit, Doc, I got 250 head out there that need to be milked and 200 acres that needs to be planted. Can't you just get me some pills to take care of this frickin problem. (pause) Time is money, you know. I can't play 20,000 questions today," he said.

"OK, George, let's check you over first." I said.

My exam continued. His blood pressure was a little elevated 140/94 and so was his pulse at 90 regular beats a minute. His neurologic exam was completely intact as was his electrocardiogram and pulmonary function. His lab tests included thyroid functions which were also normal. As the exam continued, so did my questions.

"You don't smoke or drink any alcohol, right?" I asked.

"No, but you think maybe I ought to start?" He kidded.

"How about caffeine?", I asked.

"You betcha. Usually a couple pots of coffee in the morning and then, hell, a couple of six packs of Mountain Dew in the afternoon," he said.

My eyelids rose, experiencing a transfer feeling of caffeine overload.

"That's a hell of a lot of caffeine, George," I said.

"Working 18 hours a day, you wanna try it, Doc, without a little jolt?" he said

"Can't you cut your hours back?" I asked.

He looked at me like I was from another planet. "I got kids and farmhands that don't want to work. I got my crops in early this year because I took a beating on soybeans last years. I can't get diddly squat for the price of milk these days and I owe the bank and I'm late two months payment on some equipment. Shit, cut back hours. Good luck!", he said.

"Do you get any rest and relaxation?" Iasked.

"Couple of years ago my wife and I went to Hawaii for a week," he replied. But he looked dejected as he thought of her two year struggle with uterine cancer for which I was well aware of. "She never complains, Doc. Works harder than I do." He looked me in the eyes and I nodded back.

"How's your diet besides all the caffeine you're drinking?" I asked.

"Oh, I eat but never sat down to do it." George replied.

"How about exercise?" I asked.

"Get plenty in the farm. It seems to make me feel better." George continued.

"How long are you going to keep up this pace?" I asked.

"Long as I can without losing the farm." George replied. "So, Doc, what's wrong with me?" he asked.

"Well, so far the exam and test show it may be anxiety." I replied.

He looked at me bewildered. "You mean all these symptoms are in my head. I'm no hypochondriac, you know that." George said.

"I know you're not, George, but you're under a lot of stress." I said, "If you would like a second opinion from a specialist for your peace of mind, I'll arrange for that."

George insisted on seeing a neurologist. He was worried that he was going to have a stroke. He insisted on seeing a neurologist, who could not pinpoint a problem after MRIs and EEGs. An ear, nose, and throat specialist could not verify his problem to be an inner- or middle-ear problem.

He had been consuming extraordinary amounts of caffeine in order to work 18 hours a day. He was losing his farm, and he had to sell his cows. Their family health insurance was lost. His wife, who had been treated for uterine cancer, was not out of the woods yet with that disease, and costs for her treatment were skyrocketing. Stress and anxiety over seeing most of his dreams go away had created his physical symptoms.

His family worked hard year in and year out. He had inherited the farm from his father, but it appeared most of his kids (now in their twenties) did not want to carry on the business. They saw the years of wear and tear on their father and mother, the stress and worry over paying the bills, the up and down years due to the blessings or the negative forces of mother nature, and the bureaucratic entanglement in the agriculture system by the government, which often made it hard to get an adequate price in the market.

George returned back to the office.

"Well, Doc, you were probably right. None of those expensive specialist or all of those body scans could see what was the matter with me." he said.

I nodded quietly.

"I couldn't believe it was all stress causing it." George said.

"Sometimes, you can't understand it." I added, "Probably because you're so driven to keep everything afloat and, George, you're a hard worker but everyone has their limits."

"Had to sell the cows. Auctioned them off last week." George said, misty-eyed as he hung his head staring at the floor. "Doc, my family has been milking that farm for 70 years." he said.

Seventy years. I thought of all of those generations, families and how let down he must feel.

"I'm sorry, George. What will you be doing now?" I asked.

Pathetically, with his plight, "Oh hell, there is plenty of work. I'm no welfare case and never would accept it. Probably drive truck, still grow some crops. I'm a farmer and always will be, I guess and pig-headed as always, Doc."

"George, are your symptoms improving?" I asked.

"Hell, yes. Cut out that second pot of coffee and the Mountain Dew and doing much better." George replied.

"Are you getting any more sleep, George?" I asked.

"Hell, yes. I get about 5 hours now. Better than the 3 hours I used to get." he replied.

I cringed at the thought of only getting 3-5 hours of sleep a day but some folks can do that, I guess.

"How's your wife, George?" I asked.

"Still working like a dog around the house and picked up some part time work. She'll never slow down. She has been through a cancer operation and strong as hell, Doc." he answered.

"Good to hear." I continued, "I'll see you for a check-up in 6 months, George. Good luck."

"If I stay in farming, I'm going to need a lot of luck." George chuckled.

I went to our office kitchen and poured a glass of skim milk and began to drink it. I took a second look at the glass. I always took it for granted how the milk got to this finished product. I thought of all the blood, sweat and tears that it may have taken to get it to the market that day. I really appreciated that glass of milk that day. I thought of George and the years of long hours, the risk of personal injuries, the complex market place and the forces of nature which put his crop investments at risk year after year.

George and his wife never complained. They picked up the pieces and went on. They decided not to accept social services but moved forward to find other work. They retained part of their farm to continue growing crops. Their work ethic was unshaken and the health of both did improve. They understood where they came from and kept that unshaken faith that they were in control of their own destiny.

An Unexpected Finding

———————— ◆ ————————

Moving through the day, I entered my exam room to find Mary Lou, a 19-year-old young lady who had come in to seek treatment for a respiratory infection.

"How have you been, Mary Lou" I asked, "and how's that little Amber doing?" Amber smiled and then covered her face staying shyly mute as most little ones do, probably being grateful that at 2 1/2 years old, she's not the patient today, but her mother is.

"Well, I've had this cough for a week I can't get rid of and I've been sick to my stomach." Mary Lou replied.

"How is school going? You're at the Community College, right?" I asked.

"Great." she said.

Checking her temp and listening to her chest and lungs, it was obvious she had developed bronchitis.

"Still smoking Mary Lou." I said.

"Yes, I know I gotta quit Doc." she replied.

"Better sooner than later and don't smoke around Amber." I answered.

"I try not to, Doc," she replied, "but it's hard when you live in a trailer and when it's 10 below zero at night."

"Keep trying." I replied. "So what's the complaint of nausea. How long has it been going on?" I asked.

"Couple of weeks, maybe a month." she said.

Beginning to write an antibiotic prescription, I continued, "Are you taking your birth control pills?"

"No. Haven't in two months." she replied. "I was feeling kind of queasy on them."

"Are you using any birth control?" I continued.

"Rubbers, when we remember." she said.

"Remember." I replied. "When was your last period?"

Mary Lou answered, "I haven't' had one since I stopped the pill."

"Could you give me a urine sample, Mary Lou. I want to run a pregnancy test." I said.

"Oh, you don't think I could be. Oh no, I can't be." she said. "I can't do this now."

"I'll be right back." I continued.

The test came back positive. Asking her to complete a pelvic exam. She was visibly shaken with I and my nurse present, I confirmed about a 6-8 week pregnancy. Tears rolled down the face of this woman/child with her little one comforting her for something she could not understand other than her mother's sorrow.

"I don't believe this." she lamented, "I don't know what I'm going to do. I know I should have known better."

At first, I had the inclination to agree with her, but then it dawned on me that I had no idea what her life has been like up to this point.

"Where are you living?" I asked.

"Rented trailer about 5 miles from school. My mom helps me baby-sit a couple days a week and I'm working part-time to get through school." she said.

"What about the father?" I asked.

"We're not together now. When he drinks, he gets violent and I can't have him around Amber anymore." she said, "I'm tired of getting WIC and food stamps. People look at me in the stores. I feel like dirt. I want to get through school. I really messed up this time." she said as she was shaking her head.

I pondered her predicaments.

This pregnancy was by another man than Amber's father, whom she presently did not get child support. She had dropped out of high school when she became pregnant with her first child but rebounded to get her GED and now was enrolling in a special 2-year community college program which provided day care for her child. This new pregnancy was a setback.

Sensing the failure and helplessness in her eyes, I tried to direct her in a way through which she could control her future. First, I encouraged her to stay in school at all costs and second, I referred her to a caring obstetrician who could work out with her her own personal decisions about whether she would carry this pregnancy to term or seek an abortion.

She had had no prenatal care for at least the first vital two months of embryonic development and admitted to smoking heavily and to weekend alcohol use along with "casual" drug use.

She felt ashamed of herself. Her mother had helped her with her first child, but now she wanted to be on her own. The involvement of this new father seemed highly unlikely. Counseling was available, and this she responded to.

Her family support was limited to support from her own mother, who had given birth to Mary Lou when she, too, was 17. But Mary Lou could not return home because of her father's frequent alcoholic problems; he could become quite physically and verbally abusive. Upon further questioning, I learned that the man who had impregnated her also had a drinking problem and was abusive to her.

Well, what started with a simple visit for bronchitis turned out to be a crucial turning point in the young lady's life. It is easy to find fault with her, but very wrong to follow that road. Mistakes had been made, but now the consequences were pushing her smack into a new reality.

Counseling through the state-funded community college helped her immensely to arrive at her own decisions.

The road taken would influence the rest of her life. Personal decisions with the help and guidance of others were needed. Services of WIC, Food Stamps, and Head Start for her child were utilized. This young lady needed a support system to help guide her into a more positive future for her and her child.

Several years had passed and in the room were Mary Lou and Amber.

"Hi, Doc. How's it going." Mary Lou asked.

"Good, I haven't seen you in awhile. How's Amber today?" I asked.

Amber smiled who is now nearly 5 years old.

"Good." Mary Lou said.

"Doc, I miscarried one month after I saw you, but thanks for the advice and help." Mary Lou said.

I nodded and realized how somehow nature made her decisions using her burden yet painful as it may have been at the time for her directed her to a brighter future I had hoped.

"How's school?" I asked.

"Done in May. Student teaching now." she replied.

"What grade level?" I asked.

"Nine Grade Spanish." she replied.

"Spanish, Espanol." I said, "Muy Bien! Do you like it?"

"Si." she said, "I love it. You know, Doc, I see some of those girls that I teach in ninth grade and sometimes I see myself. Some of them don't have much in the way of family life." she said.

I nodded and said, "It's sad to see this. You know how hard it is to raise a child as a teenager." I empathized with her.

"I've already talked with a few girls and told them about my daughter and working my way through college." she said.

"They need people like you, Mary Lou, in their lives." I replied.

"I guess that's why I like teaching so much." she said.

Amber was a beautiful little girl of 5, well mannered and happy at that point.

The lights in her mother and Amber's eyes were shining bright that day.

Picking Up the Pieces

———————— ◆ ————————

He was eight years old. His grandfather had brought him in for a problem with recurrent abdominal pain.

"Hi Jimmy, nice to meet you." I said.

No reply. No eye contact. Only a mild facial grimace response.

"How are you, Jack?" I asked his grandfather.

"OK, Doc. Brought my grandson in. He's been having problems with his belly." he said.

"What has been the matter?" I asked.

"Says his belly hurts a lot, especially in the morning for over three months." his grandfather replied.

"Is he having any problem moving his bowels or diarrhea." I asked.

He shrugged being unsure.

I turned to Jimmy and asked, "When was the last time you pooped?"

Jimmy shrugged his shoulders and then said, "Don't remember."

Examining Jimmy, he had no fever but his abdomen was distended and I could palpate firm masses of stool in his belly. His underwear was soiled from a chronic leakage of stool.

"Where's Jimmy's parents, Jack?" I asked.

"Jimmy and his brother are living with Mildred and I for the past couple of months. His Mom took off for Florida with another guy. I think she is heavily into drugs." Jack whispered to me, "and my son has

11

been drinking again and has not been around much to be anything of a father to Jimmy and his brother." he said dejected.

"How's his diet, energy level?" I asked.

"Hard to get him to eat his vegetables and fruits. Seems tired a lot and doesn't sleep well." Jack answered.

"How's school going for him?" I asked.

"He's falling behind in class and has trouble with obeying the rules in school." he said. "Teacher has been calling us."

After Jimmy went to the waiting room, Jack volunteered, "I never thought I'd be raising an 8 and a 6 year old aged boys in my 60's. I love these boys, so level with me if you think he has some serious problems." Jack said. "These boys have been tossed around like rag dolls for the past four years by both of their parents. Both of their parents are messed up. I somehow feel guilty my son turned out that way. I want to make it up to these boys. Mildred and I are going to give them a home. The Family Court Judge hopefully will give us full custody soon."

Jimmy was missing school and was having trouble sleeping. He often had problems with constipation and occasionally needed laxatives. Lab tests and examination revealed nothing abnormal.

His grandfather and grandmother were seeking full custody of Jimmy. His parents had been divorced for four years. Since the divorce, he and his younger brother had been with their grandparents. Their father had serious alcohol problems, and their mother had left the state with another man, she too alleged to have serious drug and alcohol problem.

Jimmy and his brother had been tossed around between their parents for years. Jimmy was very shy and didn't make eye contact easily. His grandfather noted that a change in the school year was difficult on him, especially since the custody case was being finalized. He was very sensitive to criticism and apparently was being picked on at school.

His only control through the nightmarish chain of events in his life was through his bodily functions, such as bowel control. This condition is known as encopresis, and it often results in chronic constipation and sometimes fecal impaction. His gastrointestinal problems were most likely a result of the emotional stress this young boy had been experiencing since both his parents had abandoned him.

I wondered how and why this boy deserved such an unhappy early childhood. I wondered what his life would be like and how he would turn out in his adult life. Would he some day be a substance abuser or abuse others or turn to criminal activity?

His grandparents, both retired and part-time farmers, were steadfast to raise these two boys. Without their commitment, these boys would be in an often uncertain foster care system.

With the help of school and child psychologists and a consistent life style from the grandparents, Jimmy's symptoms eventually disappeared and his performance in school improved.

Jimmy's granddad, Jack, returned for a check-up himself a few months later.

"How's Jimmy?", I asked.

"Good, Doc. He and his brother are doing great. School is going better and he's playing sports." he continued, "Mildred and I keep them busy around the house, too. It seems like all those boys needed was some sort of consistent lifestyle, some self-discipline and self-control. I never could believe a mother could walk away from her kids. My son has been trying a lot more, but he still has a big problem, Doc. I think with the booze, when he's not working. He moves around a lot as a trucker, sometimes on the road coast to coast for three weeks. Doc, I'll never understand where I failed him and I'll never understand why people can't put their children first in their priority of life." Jack said.

I nodded to Jack and said, "Jack, you would be surprised how many folks I know that are raising their grandchildren."

"What in the hell is going on in the world?" Jack said. "Don't these people know that when they get married and have kids that marriage isn't a 50/50 proposition, it's not a 'what's in it for me'. It's 100/100% proposition. I guess they just want to satisfy their needs first."

I quietly shook my head in agreement and admiration to a man that couldn't complain about his unexpected parenting role in his late 60's.

"Doc, they are our flesh and blood and I can't believe my son and the boy's mom can live with themselves. I guess they don't care or feel anything. Probably too numb from all the crap they've done to themselves over the years." Jack said.

"Jack, just think if you and Mildred weren't there to take care of these boys. They'd probably be moving through Foster homes and there would be a chance they would be either juvenile criminals or exposed to drugs and alcohol at a very young age. These boys are fortunate to have you as grandparents." I said.

"No, Doc, we're fortunate to have them." Jack smiled, nearly teary eyed.

I thought about all those children whose parents had virtually abandoned them. Sometimes leaving them with grandparents, aunts and uncles. I thought how important it was for them to have a consistent structured and loving environment that gives them self-discipline and self-control. That is what eventually cured Jimmy's problems.

We all have a stake in reaching these goals. Hats off to Jimmy and especially to his grandparents. These fine people still felt responsible for their son's failure, but they also knew their responsibility to their grandsons, that these boys were their flesh and blood. Their love for these children would never take second place. The pieces had been picked up and put back in place.

Never a Complainer

◆

"Hi, Doc. How's the family?" Don smiled.

"Good, Don. Nice to see you this morning." I replied.

"Beautiful day. Passed a doe and her fawns in the field. Pretty sight." Don said.

"Let's see, you need your blood pressure checked and medicine renewed and its time for your annual physical." I said.

"Sounds good." he said.

"How's farming going?" I asked.

"Got a lot of crops in. May be last season." He replied.

"Oh really." I said.

"Yeah, time to call it quits and enjoy life. Maybe winter in Florida with the Mrs. Probably gonna sell to this nice young Mennonite family." he said

"Sounds good, Don. You deserve it." I said. "Let's finish the exam and make sure you leave me a urine sample before you leave the office and we gotta get your weight yet. OK?"

"OK." he replied.

"There's blood in your urine." After I looked under the microscope, I spoke bluntly with Dan, a farmer who had dairy cows but grew hundreds of acres of grain and feed for decades. It was a significant amount of blood. Except for this, Don appeared very healthy, except that e had lost five pounds since his last visit and stated he was a little tired.

15

This man was from stock that said little, never complained, and worked 16 hours daily, sometimes seven days a week. He was one of those "salt of the earth" folks whom I and my staff respected and revered.

"What do you think's causing it , Doc" , I haven't noticed any pain or bleeding, never had any kidney stones either " Don stated.

Well Don , it could be a number of things. I would like to get some tests which would include an IVP ,that is a special x-ray of your kidneys and urinary tract, and a renal sonogram and if we need to we will consult with a urologist and possibly have you get a cystoscopy which is a direct look inside your bladder" I answered carefully.

"Think it could be cancer , Doc " ? Don solemnly asked as our eyes locked as if he had already read my thoughts.

"Don, cancer is something we are going to have to rule out. But let's not jump the gun until all the tests are completed, OK" I replied.

"OK Doc , but could we hold off til I get my fields harvested next month, lots of things I gotta do before Winter comes" Don asked?

" No Don, let's get these tests done right away, better safe than sorry" I replied

" OK Doc , your the boss" Don grinned.

The IVP revealed a suspicious bladder lesion and Don had to undergo a cystoscopy. It revealed a large bladder cancer.

Don returned for his pre-op clearance physical.

"Well Doc, got more than I bargained for I guess". Don muttered in a rare moment of dejection.

"Are you getting some help with your crops ,Don"? I asked.

"Oh my sons and neighbors have helped me a lot Doc, thank the good Lord , Don't know what I'd do without them". Don answered

"Thats great Don". I continued. Well Don, I know Dr. Keiser has discussed with you the procedure He will have to perform. You will have an Ileal pouch made from a section of your small intestines to replace your diseased bladder and then"

Don interjected. " Doc , think I'll have chemo"?

"We will have to discuss that with the cancer specialist once we can figure out how far the cancer has advanced and we will know this after surgery and after the results of the pathology results on lymph nodes removed from your pelvic and abdominal region." I answered, hoping that I didn't sound too removed from Don's present plight.

"I appreciate all that you and the other doctors have done for me , sometimes your job isn't easy". Don replied

I was overwhelmed that a man faced with a possible fatal disease could actually turn it around and express empathy for those that were helping him . What a lesson this man was for others.

" Thanks Don". I said and as we shook hands I only wondered and wished that he had shown up six months earlier. Could I have caught this cancer in its earlier stages?

Don did well with his surgery. He had the ileal conduit attached to his ureters and would have to wear an ostomy bag to collect his urine.

Dons ' pathology reports on his lymph nodes revealed an aggressive metastatic cancer. Don immediately began a combination of chemotherapy drugs.

In the next three months Don became a familiar face at the oncologists office. Don stopped by my office for a routine follow up. His hair was gone and he had lost about fifteen pounds.

"Hi Doc, How's the family"? Don smiled.

"Great Don, good to see you". I paused, " It's been quite a rocky road far you".

"Well , it wasn't where I expected to be but that's life Doc". Don replied.

"Are you having much nausea or pain"? Do you or your wife need any assistance at home"?I asked.

"No Doc , thanks for askin, but I'm still working the farm. I've cut my hours back some. Don't really like to take pain pills , dulls the senses. I'll let you know if The day comes when I may need them. Right now the cancer doctor and his assistants are doing a good job keeping my nausea down on the day that I have chemo'. Don answered.

Don continued " I have this suspicion that being around pesticides and herbicides all my life had something to do with this cancer. I used a lot of sprays , especially twenty years ago , when there was a lot less warnings. Hell, one of my neighbors thinks I should sue the chemical manufacturer for causing my cancer . Hell Doc, Sue!" Don chuckled. " I'm not made like that. I should have known better and taken more precautions when I was around that stuff. All these people are sue crazy, not willing to take any responsibility for their own actions." Don exclaimed.

"I know what you mean Don". I continued , " We also do not have enough information about all the chemicals used in agriculture, but one thing is for sure, many of these chemicals can remain and accumulate in your body over the years sand that could lead to cancer. Don I wish we could have found this earlier ."I said in a somber state.

"Doc , you did your best and remember I didn't know it either. " Don answered.

A year had passed. Dons' cancer had spread. His weight loss was marked. His renal and cardiac function had deteriorated from the intense onslaught of chemotherapy . He was experiencing daily , if not constant pain and he finally gave into pain medication. My last visit with Him revealed a body given in to the rage of an all consuming disease but the peace in his eyes revealed a spirit fulfilled.. Don had always had a steadfast inner peace. He knew who he was . He understood his connection with the world that he was part of. He accepted his death in the same manner in which he appreciated life.

Don never complained. Perhaps he had wished he had taken greater care with the toxic exposures of the past decades. But he accepted his illness gracefully, and somehow the strength of his character grew even more in helping his family and friends cope with their loss when his day finally came.

Not Ritalin

◆

Jimmy sat quietly on the exam table. His mom sat with her arms crossed, tapping her feet nervously. "Doctor, Jimmy's hyperactive. He's always getting in fights with his brother and has been getting into trouble in school recently," she continued. "I was hoping you could prescribe Ritalin for him; it has helped one of my best friends' kids a lot."

I was beginning to sense that she was not going to take "no" for an answer.

"How are you, Jimmy? Let's see, you're in 6th no 7th grade, right?" I asked.

"Uh huh. 7th grade." Jimmy replied.

"Do you like school, Jimmy?" I asked.

"It's boring," he replied, sitting quite still and obviously not wanting to be here.

Turning to his mom, I questioned, "How is he doing in school before this year?"

She replied, "OK, I guess. He usually gets B's. It's hard to get him to do his homework but this year he is terrible and he's falling behind and getting disciplined in school."

"Does he work well on his own. Can he carry out a task OK. Can he follow directions OK?" I asked.

"Only unless its something he really wants to do." his mother said.

"What do you like to do, Jimmy?" I asked.

"Stuff, computer. I like the Internet." he replied.

"Do you spend a lot of time on it?" I asked.

"Guess so, it's kind of neat." he said.

His mother added, "Hours. Can't get him off of it and then he likes to channel surf on the TV."

"Does he get fidgety, restless, talks without thinking or seems extremely overactive?" I asked.

"Only sometimes, but not always. I guess not." his mother continued as she thought.

"Is he having problems obeying rules in school?" I asked.

"Uh-huh." said his mother affirmatively.

"No-oo." replied Jimmy to his mother in a fresh manner.

"How are you getting along with your classmates, Jimmy?" I asked.

"A couple of kids are bugging me." he said.

"He's getting in fights; been twice to the principal's office and detention once." his mother replied.

"Are you making any new friends this year, Jimmy?" I asked.

"Yeah, I suppose a couple." Jimmy said.

His mother intervened and showed me notes from his teachers. The note said, "Something seems to be bothering Jimmy. His work is slacked-off and he seems to be less interested in school and he has had to be disciplined more for not paying attention. This is quite a change from last year's teacher evaluation.

"Are you still in boyscouts, going camping this summer, Jimmy?" I asked.

"I don't know. My dad can't be scout master. He's working a lot of hours." he answered.

"He and his dad used to hike and camp all year round. It's been a rough year financially and Mark had to take a second job. He's on the road a lot so that hasn't happened lately. A lengthy sheet of questions were handed to Jimmy's mother with instructions for his teachers to fill out regarding possible Attention Deficit Disorder.

"So, Doc, what about Ritalin?" his mother asked.

"Not yet. Let's look at the response from the teacher's evaluation, it is very important, and I don't want to start a long-term drug if I don't have to. OK? It's in his best interest." I replied.

She seemed a little taken back but was willing to wait.

Jimmy was 13 and had never been referred before for evaluation of attention-deficit disorder. In fact, school performance had been fine until this year. Jimmy's mom, however, stated that he always had a short attention span when he wasn't interested in something.

After a lengthy history review, it became obvious that Jimmy did not have a disorder of hyperactivity or attention deficit that would require a psychostimulant such as Ritalin.

Ritalin has proven to be quite successful in children that are properly screened. Many of these children's behavior problems are picked up in grade school, and medication helps school performance quite remarkably.

Sitting with Jimmy's mom, after she had returned. We reviewed the teacher's questionnaire on Attention Deficit Disorder.

"Well, Mary, it looks as if Jimmy really doesn't fit the criteria for hyperactivity, attention deficit." I said.

Mary, at first, sat with her arms and legs crossed.

"What am I going to do with him? He is driving my nuts." she said.

"Mary, have things been rougher since Jim's dad had to take a second job? Do you think Jimmy's behavior has been a lot worse since that point?" I asked.

"They spent so much time together before. It really bothers my husband that he can't be home more but they cut his hours and pay at his other job, so he has to be out on the road with his second job working weekends." She answered.

"So, is Jimmy filling his time now in front of a television or computer?" I asked.

"I guess you're right about that, Doc." she answered.

"Turn them off." I said.

"He'll have a conniption, Doc." she said.

"Try getting back to the things that you all used to enjoy doing together and get Jimmy focused on creative things that he likes to do." I said.

"You're right, I've got to get him back to some projects, back to his piano and other things." she said.

"Maybe some projects you can do together. It will help him keep focused on it." I said.

Mary left in a state of wondering how she is going to do this but willing to give it a try.

One month had passed. Jimmy came in with his dad., Mark.

"Hi, Mark. Jimmy, how's it going?" I asked.

"Good." Jimmy said.

"Very good." Mark said as he showed me Jimmy's report card and teacher's comment.

"Doc, I cut back my hours and spend more time at home on weekends. There was a lot of stress going on awhile back but things are getting better." Mark said.

"What have you been up to, Jimmy?" I asked.

"Well, we were on a fishing trip last weekend and next month we're heading on to the Adirondaks for a week canoeing." Jimmy answered.

"Great. It's beautiful up there." I said. "I hope you enjoy it."

"Took your advice. Mary and I turned off the computer and television as much as we can." Mark said.

"Sounds like you've got other things to keep you busy, Jimmy." I said. He smiled.

It was heartwarming to see a smile from this young boy that three months ago, people were considering Ritalin for. I was wondering how many children have lived this way with little time for family interaction and creative playing.

"Mark, it always frightens me when children or teenagers spend most of their time in front of a TV or computer monitor. It leaves little time in the real world." I said.

He nodded and replied, "I know."

A "mediaectomy" was performed on Jimmy and the operation was a complete success.

Ritalin was not the answer here.

A Pleasant Repetition

◆

"Hi, Norma. How was your winter in Florida?" I asked.

"Not so good, Doc. It's Albert, he's really slipping." she replied.

"How so?" I asked.

"Can't remember one thing from the next. He follows me around all day asking the same questions. He's driving me crazy." Norma sobbed.

"It's been awhile since Albert's been in for a check-up. He's not on any meds, no recent acute illnesses. He missed his last two check-up appointments last year and the year before. Let's see, nearly three years, I guess, Norma. We'll check him over real well." I said.

"Doc, he tried mowing the lawn yesterday, just kept riding the tractor around in the same circle, made a real nice path but he never cut the grass." Norma said.

"How is he at night, Norma?" I asked.

"Sometimes OK. Sometimes he wanders and I have to lead him back to bed. He gets really mixed up. Doc, I took all the ammo out of the house. Al used to be quite the hunter. Now he scares the Be-Jesus out of me. Don't trust his judgment." Norma said.

"OK, Norma. Let me see Albert and we'll probably order some tests to correctly understand the change in his mental state." I said.

"Doc, he was a sharp fella. He ran his own little electronics business for years and sold out to enjoy his retirement years. Well, here we are, but he's not here." She said.

I entered the room to see Albert after talking with Norma.

"How are you doing today, Doc?" A very pleasant elderly man (whom I have not seen in three year) was in for his routine visit. What seemed like a pleasant greeting was notably taken as part of his disorder. It was now the fourth time he had said the same phrase in about fifteen minutes after I was in and out of the exam room talking with his wife and taking some telephone calls. He was unaware that he had repeated himself four times.

"Albert, how was your winter?" I asked.

"Good, real good." he said.

With Norma present, I continued, "Albert, I'm going to ask you some questions and I'd like you to try to answer them. OK?"

"OK, Doc." he said.

I asked, " What is the year?"

"Uh," Albert said, "Nineteen (pause) fifty (pause) two."

I continued, "What season is it?"

"Let's see, it's spring." he replied correctly.

"What month is it, Albert?" I asked.

"Uh, October, no November." he said.

"What town is this?" I asked.

"It's Cato." he correctly answered and his wife sighed a little relief.

"What State are you in?" I asked.

"New York." Albert answered correct again.

I continued, "I want you to name three objects and now listen carefully and repeat after me and then I want you to try to remember these three objects because I'm going to ask them again. Ready, Albert?" I asked.

"OK." he said.

"Apple, table and penny." I replied.

"Apple, table. What was the last one?" Albert said.

"Penny." I said.

"Penny." he said.

"Can you spell world backwords?"I continued.

Albert answered, "W-umm." Then he stopped.

Norma interrupted, "No, Albert, backwards, spell it backwards!" in an anxious tone.

I cautioned Norma to try to remain silent. She was growing frustrated and wanted to spell it herself.

Albert tried, "L-D-" and then fell silent.

"Albert can you name those three objects I asked you to remember?" I said.

"Uh...world...um" and then, again, fell silent. Albert stopped.

"No, Albert, those three words, apple, penny, table." Norma yelled frustrated that this once fast thinker couldn't do a simple memory game.

"It's OK, Norma," I said, "let's continue."

I showed Albert my pen and my watch and asked him to name them.

"Pen and...time" he said.

"Albert, can you take a paper in your right hand, fold it in half and put in on the floor." I asked.

Albert picked up the piece of paper with his right hand and put it on the floor forgetting to fold it.

"Albert, can you subtract 7 from 100?" I asked.

Albert thought, "Ninety...three."

"Good, good." I said.

"Can you subtract 7 from that number" I asked.

Albert tried, "Seventy...six."

"Seven from that number." I asked.

Albert fell silent, not answering.

My exam did not reveal any evidence of neurologic focal deficits one would see from a series of strokes, nor any evidence of Parkinson's Disease. His blood pressure and EKG were normal. His labs were drawn and his blood sugar, electrolytes, thryroid function, B12 levels and sed rate were normal. An MRI of the brain was ordered which showed atrophy, especially in the temporal and parietal regions of the brain but no obvious large strokes, tumors or excessive fluid in the brain. Except for his failing cognitive function, Albert was a very healthy specimen at 75 years of age.

Albert had moderately advanced Alzheimer's disease. His short-term memory was all but gone. He was unable to add or subtract accurately. His wife, Norma, had noticeably lost some weight, painfully told me of his persistent paranoid behavior, how often he would follow her around the house, repeating himself over and over. When nighttime arrived, it was important to keep the bedroom light lit, or he would often become confused and sometimes combative, wandering through the house and sometimes outside.

I conveyed my test results to Norma.

"Norma, do you get any help, any of the family around?" I asked.

"No, my son is in California. Got a great job and busy life with his wife and 3 kids. My daughter and her family are in North Carolina." she replied.

"Norma, Albert has Alzheimer's Disease, I believe." I said.

Norma already knew, but sighed a relief about knowing that she pursued the necessary avenues just in case something could be reversed.

"I know, Doc. Been doing a lot of reading lately. I guess I've known it for a long time. I wish I could have convinced him to get in to see you a couple of years ago." she said.

"Sometimes, in the early years of this disorder, Albert and folks with this disorder can cover their tracks pretty good." I said.

"He did, Doc. But, I guess, I did too for him." she answered tearfully.

For the past five years, his wife now noted a gradual deterioration with his behavior and forgetfulness. It was now approaching the time that she needed respite help as the weariness and despair was obvious in her eyes.

As in any other family, folks in the country try to maintain their loved ones at home sometimes sacrificing all of themselves to an incredible degree.

After an extensive workup for dementia, including various blood tests and MRIs, Alzheimer's was diagnosed by exclusion. Within a year, he would need proprietary home care, and in two years nursing home care. He was 76 years old and could live another five years.

He was a successful owner of a small business and had retired comfortably in his late 60s. A once very meticulous and self-confident man had been cruelly reduced to a life where dignity had been gradually stripped away, and the disease had taken its toll on his spouse.

Different medications were tried, including Cognex and Aricept, with limited success. The future for Albert is not promising.

"Norma wants to talk to you." my Nurse pointed to Room 3.

I entered the room. Norma was sitting quietly in her usual meticulous nature always well-dressed and immaculately groomed.

"It has been getting tougher." she said. "He has been quite combative."

"We'll try Risperdal along with the Aricept to see if it will keep him calm. Are you getting any help, Norma?" I asked.

"An Aide comes in for a couple of hours a day." she replied.

"Are you getting an sleep, Norma?" I asked.

"When I can. He sleeps OK most of the time." she answered.

"Have you thought about assisted living for Albert, Norma?" I asked.

"Doc, it's $3,000.00 a month and forget about a Nursing Home. We'll be bankrupt. In this day and age, if your mind goes first, you spend your way into poverty and then the government pays the rest. It seems like those long-term care policies sound great, but who can afford them and who would ever know that Albert would have lost his mind 7 years ago." she said.

I sensed her predicament.

"The emotional and financial stress are tough on you right now." I said.

"Doc, I'll let you in on a secret. I packed Albert's bags one morning and took him up to Northbrook after a really rough evening. I got him checked in and into his room. I started crying, unpacked his bags and then packed them up again and took him home. I couldn't leave him there. We came home that same day. After all we've been through, I couldn't leave him like this." she said.

"Please try to get more help at home and let's see if some medications can ease his agitation." I said.

"Someday, Norma, I hope and pray we can find a cure for this terrible disorder." I said.

"I'm afraid it's too late for Albert, Doc." she said.

I nodded and said, "I know. I wish I could do more."

"You've done the best you can, Doc. Albert would appreciate that." she said.

"So have you, Norma. So have you." I said.

As the years passed, Albert eventually entered a skilled nursing home. Every day, his wife, Norma, would sit at his bedside, feeding him, bathing him, reading to him, and soothing him. Hours on end, seven days a week. Norma was one who understood the meaning of unconditional love as do the millions of caretakers for folks with this disease.

Not His Time

◆

I was traveling to the hospital at 6 a.m. to see a patient. A heavy March rain had left a thick fog on this dark, dreary morning.

I was called in to see an elderly fellow who showed up in the emergency room with abdominal pain and a fever of 104?. After introducing myself to Bob, I proceeded, "How long have you had pain?"

"What, speak up." he moaned.

"How long have you had your belly pain?" I replied, quite louder realizing he was quite hearing impaired.

"When did it start to rain?" he said. Rescued by the patient's wife, she intervened, "Doc, I think it started after dinner but he wouldn't get in the car and come to the hospital until my son and daughter-in-law carried him into their car. Bob hates hospitals and doesn't particularly care for doctors. Hasn't seen one in 25 years."

"Ah, this cussin pain." he moaned.

I proceeded to examine him and look at the abdominal films. It was apparent that he had severe bowel obstruction.

I said, yelling, "Bob, Dr. Ryan's been called in. He's a fine surgeon and he's going to have to operate to relieve a blockage in your bowel."

Bob replied, "I he gets rid of this pain, he can do what he wants. Let's get on with it."

Consents were signed by his wife and family as he was obviously getting weaker.

A surgical consult was called in, and concurred with a diagnosis of an acute bowel obstruction, and emergency surgery was performed.

I had known his wife and children well but had never met Bob. Here was a 76-year-old fellow still working every day from dawn to dusk as a dairy farmer who had never sought medical care. He was notably hearing impaired, and the years of hard labor showed in his markedly arthritic hands and knees. His black hair, though, had never grayed. He had a face that appeared chiseled out by the years of sun and wind—the long, hot days of summer and the bone chilling January mornings leaving their impressions. His eyes, which I would later grow to know as quite fierce and to the point, now were beleaguered and resigned on this particular damp March morning.

Surgery went successfully, but a serious bacterial infection, that began prior to the surgery, developed due to the fact that his stubborn nature delayed an earlier intervention. He remained on life support in intensive car for 30 days as he lay in an unresponsive coma.

Multiple specialists—including neurologists, cardiologists, a pulminologist, and an infectious disease consultant performed numerous diagnostic tests and tried multiple regimens of drug therapy.

Not being of any particular denomination, his lovely wife, also with years of disabling arthritis, invited any clergy who offered to to pray over him. She said, "We would take any help we could get from above." Priests, ministers, and rabbis all gave him their blessing. His family stayed steadfast with him.

Finally, I decide to try a new antibiotic, even against the advice of a few specialists. Well, he surprisingly woke up two days later. After a few days, he was taken off the ventilator. The first day he spoke, after having his tracheostomy covered and in a disoriented state, he said, "Those nurses are trying to force me to smoke marijuana."

After being on a ventilator for a month, Bob had to plug his temporary tracheostomy to tell me that.

"Bob, how are you?" I asked, noting his hearing aid was in.

"Who the hell are you?" he spoke up.

"I'm your doctor, been attending to you since you've been a patient here after surgery." I said.

"Tell those nurses that they can't make me smoke that funny stuff and neither can you." he said.

"Don't worry, Bob, I think you'll be safe." I said.

"Where the hell am I anyway?" he asked.

"You're in the hospital, Bob. Auburn Hospital and had surgery and you were very sick. You've been here a month in a coma but you have somehow come out of it." I said.

"When can I get out of here?" he asked.

"It won't be long." I said. "Get some rest and I'll see you tomorrow."

I had to laugh and wonder how he ever got that idea, or whether he had had a hemp crop in past years. This was my first verbal contact with him since his coma.

The next day, he spoke again grabbed me with his very firm, labored hands by my stethoscope and pulled me cloase and asked me, "Why the hell did you bother to keep me alive?"

"Aren't you glad to be awake and getting better and going home soon?" I asked.

"What for." he said, "Shoulda let me die." he replied.

"What about your wife and family?" I asked.

"Oh hell, better off without me. I ain't no good to anyone. Got bad wheels with this damned arthritis. Slows me down and hurts like hell." he replied.

"Maybe we can help you with your pain, so you feel a little better." I said.

He looked at me with distant eyes and a strong hint of depression.

"Let's get some physical therapy going for your. You've been bed-ridden for a month and then lets get you out of here and back on your tractor. OK, Bob?" I said.

He nodded and closed his eyes.

Well, what was a brief period of medical ego enhancement for me quickly floundered. I fought to help keep him alive for one month and this was his gratitude. I shook my head all the way during my drive from the hospital to my office, 20 miles away. Then, the sun popped through the clouds in the eastern sky. It dawned on me, at that point, that it was his life and his decision to make. He may not have wanted to live because his body was wearing down. His life was a life of hard labor that he couldn't do much of anymore. Maybe it was supposed to be his time and I interfered. Was it my right to do that? I though of the cost, probably $100,000.00 to keep him going, most of it paid by Medicare and Medicaid. I thought of all of those people in Intensive Care Units on life support that never expressed their wishes prior to their catastrophic illness.

Bob went home and recuperated though. He gimped in with his cane two weeks later. It was planting time and I was wondering if he was going to be right back out there.

"Hi, Bob. Hi, Wilma. How are you?" I asked.

"We're fine." Wilma said as she smiled.

Bob said nothing. Looking kind of mean.

"Well, let's check you over, Bob. How's the bowels working?" I asked.

"They ain't without this liquid crap." Bob answered.

He was referring to Lactulose, a liquid medicine that often helps his bowels stay regular.

"How's the arthritis, Bob?" I asked.

"Can't get a cussed thing done. Moving in slow motion." Bob answered and continued, "and I'm still getting all those Specialist bills. I never met one of them sons a bitches except you and Dr. Ryan."

"I hope I wasn't one of those sons-a-bitches, Bob." I said.

He smiled for the first time. It made my day.

"Doc, those arthritis pills help a little." Bob said.

"Good, Bob." I said and continued, "I wanted to talk to you about completing paperwork that would express your desire, if you ever needed life support treatment again. This is a Health Care Proxy form for which designates another person to direct your medical decision-making in case you are unable to do so. This other form expresses your desire to give, in advance, a directive over what type of medical and life support you so desire in case you are, again, unable to make any kind of decisions regarding this. Whether you wanted to be maintained on life support such as a respirator to keep you alive. The final form is a Do Not Resuscitate Order to put in your chart. That would mean that we would not do any cardiac, pulmonary resuscitation in case your heart stopped. Do you understand this."

Bob nodded, grabbed my pen with his twisted, arthritic fingers and asked, "Where do I sign?"

While he was signing he said, chuckling, "Next time they plan to take me to the hospital better to just take me out in the back of the barn and shoot me."

Wilma shook her head saying, "I think I'll put blanks in the gun. That will scare him when I point it at him."

We all laughed knowing they weren't serious.

Heading home one fragrant, Spring afternoon with the apple blossoms in full bloom, I spotted Bob riding his tractor, plowing the fields for the feed crop. I beeped but he didn't have a clue who I was, he just kept on going. He was alive and content in his world and doing what he loved to do. Those kind of things you can't put a price tag on, I guess.

It was not his time to die.

The Valium of the Nineties

———◆———

A young man in his early thirties came in. I had known Joe as a hard working school teacher who had been having trouble sleeping as of late.

"How long have you been having trouble sleeping?" I asked.

"Long time, maybe a year." he answered.

"Do you have any difficulty falling asleep or do you wake up and can't get back to sleep?" I continued.

"Seems like I sleep until 2 a.m., then I'm up pacing the floor. Some real bad television on at that time, Doc." he answered.

"How do you feel each morning?" I asked.

"Well what do you expect, no energy, tired as hell and can't concentrate worth a damn on my job and I'm also losing my patience in school." he said.

"Work's not going so well. Are you still coaching?" I asked.

"Didn't feel like it much this year. I guess I lost interest." he said.

"Has your mood been down, do you feel you don't laugh much?" I asked.

"Doc, I'm embarrassed to say, but I feel like crying a lot. Broke up with my lady friend about 6 months ago and she moved out. We were having problems for a long time.

"I see, sorry to hear that Joe." I said.

"How's your appetite? Have you been losing weight?" I asked.

"Lost about 15 pounds. Some days, I just forget to eat much." Joe answered.

"Do you drink alcohol or use drugs?" I asked.

"Hell no. I've seen too many friends mess their lives up with those things, Doc." he answered.

"You're still pretty close with your family; your parents and your brother's family?" I asked.

"Yeah. They're great." he said.

"Do have feelings of restlessness and are you irritable around other people?" I asked.

"I've been a son of a bitch lately. It doesn't take much to make me fly off the handle." he said.

"How do you feel about your future?" I asked.

"I don't know." he said.

"Joe, have you ever thought of taking your life?" I asked.

Joe gasped, hung his head down, his eyes watered.

"A few months ago I thought seriously about it but realized that I could never do this to my parents and my family." he answered.

"What thoughts did you have, Joe? Did you have any actual plan? Joe, do you own a gun?" I asked.

"Yes, I've hunted all my life, but it never occurred to me and I couldn't do it. I just thought about being dead, but realized I would never consider it because of what it would do to my folks. Couldn't come close to that." Joe volunteered.

"OK, Joe. I understand and I'm glad you told me." I said.

"Have you felt down just since the break-up with your lady friend or before that?" I asked.

"I think I've always been a little down, but after she left, I felt more alone and more down." he answered.

"Joe, would you agree to see a counselor to work out some of these issues?" I asked.

"I guess I could. Not a shrink, I hope, I don't need someone thinking that I'm crazy. I'm not crazy, you know." he said.

"I know that, Joe. But I think it would help. I also wonder if an anti-depressant medication might help you. It would take about two weeks to notice a difference." I said.

We reviewed the potential side effects and he agreed to try it.

"I'll see you in two weeks. Here's my phone number. Call if you have any questions or problems." I said.

"OK, Doc. I'll give it a try." he said.

Joe returned for his two week follow-up visit.

"I didn't take the medicine you prescribed; I heard it turned you into a touchy-feely kind of person, and I'm not that kind of guy." Laughing in response, I sensed a smile in this young teacher. Two weeks earlier, I'd determined after an extended visit that he was very depressed.

He had at first been very embarrassed to come in to see me for this problem. He had not been sleeping well. He had ended a relationship about six months before and felt isolated. He couldn't concentrate well at work and was flying off the handle at things he couldn't believe he was getting upset about. He had denied any suicide attempts but had had a few thoughts about it a few months back. He had confided that he could neither do such a thing to his parents nor leave them with the memory of a suicide.

On his first visit, he had made little or no eye contact and had not been able to laugh much. After careful screening and history taking, a trial of Prozac had been discussed along with counseling.

Joe pursued counseling and self-help literature, but decided not to undergo drug therapy. On his follow-up visit, he seemed more confident in his demeanor and somewhat more at ease with himself.

I respected his decision and encouraged him to continue his counseling with my door remaining open.

Three months had passed.

"Hi, Joe. How are you feeling?" I asked.

"Hi, Doc. Just in for a sinus infection. Think I'll need some antibiotics." he said.

"OK, Joe. How are things going compared to last time you were here?" I asked.

"Good, good. Much better." he replied.

"No problems with sleep or irritability or anxiety?" I asked.

"Doing better. I cut down on caffeine and started exercising a lot more. Reading up on some good books. Thanks for the information." he said.

"Sometimes, it's hard for people to come in to seek counseling and sometimes it's harder for men than woman to admit some help is needed or that some changes are needed. I know it was hard coming in." I said.

"At first, I wanted to try the antidepressants but, the more I read and the more I looked around, I couldn't believe how many people were taking antidepressants such as friends and other teachers, college professors. Depression is pretty widespread." he said.

"Some people really do benefit from these medications." I said, "But I guess with anything, it might be overprescribed to some who may not need it but also might help those who do not seek help." I said.

"Kind of like Valium was a few years back." Joe stated.

I thought about what he said knowing that Valium was not the same drug as the new antidepressants but there was some validity in what he said. Valium was prescribed for millions of people showing anxiety symptoms, suppressing their symptoms. Now, it is time for these new drugs in the 90's and depression seems quite common. I wonder how much was prescribed inappropriately before other non-drug therapies were attempted.

"I guess there is some truth to that, Joe." I replied.

"How is school going?" I asked.

"Oh, much better. I'm going to coach this Spring." he said.

"Great." I said.

"Also, I met a real great gal. Things are going good." he said.

"Well, things are better than the last time." I said.

"Got to keep plugging. Counseling has really helped as has exercising hard 5 days a week". he said.

"I'm glad to hear you're doing this without medications. Keep in touch and I'll see you soon." I said.

I looked at all the samples the drug reps had left in my office. Competing with the other drug companies for their market share of the Depression Bonanza. I realized it doesn't take a lot to write a prescription and, how often the underlying conditions that lead to depression are never addressed. Therapy with medication alone without resolution of internal and external conflict is a quick and temporary fix. How important solid relationships were in overcoming depression.

Joe had worked hard to overcome his problems. He reached deep within himself to find the light that overcame his darkness.

A Stomach Ache

◆

Mark complained that he was living on Tagament and Tums daily. "Doc, you gotta treat my ulcer." Considering his diagnosis and further testing, I first observed him. He appeared disheveled and had obviously been losing weight except for his enlarged belly. His muscle tone appeared to be poor and wasting. His face was bloated, with a ruddy nose and complexion. His eyes had a hint of jaundice, with a sense of anger or despair.

"Mark, how long have you been having stomach problems?" I asked.

"On and off for a couple of months. Really bad last week. I'm eating bottles of Tums and popping Tagamet over-the-counter." he said.

"Does it bother you all the time or mostly before or after meals?" I asked.

"Mostly all the time, Doc." he replied.

"How's the rest of you been doing, Mark?" I asked.

"What do you mean?" he replied.

"How's the job at the power plant?" I asked.

"OK. Some hassles with the boss. I've got to get an excuse for work. I missed the last two days on account of my stomach problems." he said.

"How's the family?" I asked.

"My ex has the kids, been divorced two years. I see them now and then." he said.

"Sorry to hear that." I said.

"Mark, are you still smoking?" I asked.

"Can't quit 'em, Doc." he said.

"How much?" I asked.

"A couple of packs a day. Smoking lights though." he answered.

I nodded as if it really made a difference in a sarcastic sense.

"Drinking much?" I asked.

"Yeah, some." he replied.

"How much in a day do you usually drink?" I asked.

"A couple of beers. Hardly any hard stuff." he answered.

"How many beers would you really, on average, go through in a day?" I asked.

"Week nights, maybe eight. Weekends, who knows, quite a bit more." he replied.

"You drink at home lately since that DWI that you had a couple of years ago?" I asked.

"That son-of-bitch sheriff gave me the shaft. Said I blew 1.4. Bullshit. I only had a couple and got stopped in a road block." he said.

"Mark, have you ever felt the need to cut down on your drinking?" I asked.

"Sometimes, I guess, after a long weekend. But, overall, I can handle my beer." he said.

"Have people ever annoyed you by criticizing your drinking?" I asked.

"My ex annoyed me to no end. Probably a good reason we're not together." he said.

"Have you ever felt bad or guilty about drinking?" I asked.

"Why do you ask?" he snapped back, getting a little antsy.

"I just wanted to see if I could help you." I continued.

"I came her to get some help for my stomach. You think I'm some major skid row alky?" he asked.

"No," I said, "most alcoholics are not skid row, they're from all walks of life."

"What about my stomach. Are you going to help me?" Mark asked.

I turned and looked him right straight in the eye and asked, "Do you think your alcohol consumption is causing your stomach problems?"

"I don't know, do you?" he said.

"Yes, I do." I said honestly.

"One more question, Mark. Do you take morning eye openers to steady your nerves or get rid of a hangover?" I asked.

"Only on weekend, not on work days." he answered.

"OK, let me examine you and we'll need to obtain a few diagnostic tests.

He had been divorced for two years. Probing further, he stated he usually consumed three to four beers a day. Asking further, the number rose to a case every other day. He was smoking two packs daily. He was fighting a recent DWI, which he said wasn't his fault and the officer harassed him. This man's life was an absolute mess and denial of his alcoholism was quite obvious.

Further evaluation revealed a palpably enlarged liver and some loss of sensation in his toes. He had advanced physical signs of alcohol neuropathy, liver disease, and gastritis. He had recently missed a lot of work from his factory job and was really in today to get a medical excuse. Lab tests showed elevated, abnormal liver function tests.

"Mark, I've reviewed your lab reports and your labs show elevated liver fucntions and your liver sonogram shows a fatty liver. You have no ulcer, only gastritis. Your exam shows, you have some nerve damage from excessive alcohol use. I believe all of your symptoms are caused by severe irritation to your esophagus and stomach and also now appears your liver is becoming severely damaged by your alcohol intake." I replied.

"OK, Doc, I can handle the alcohol." he said.

"I hope you understand, that you have to quit entirely." I said.

He rolled his eyes and said, "I'll cut down, I can handle it."

"Your alcohol problem may actually require more aggressive inpatient treatment counseling and Alcoholics Anonymous." I said.

"You're shittin' me, aren't ya? My problems are not that bad." Mark replied.

"I'm not." I said.

"Well, I ain't going. Got too many bills to pay. I'm back on child support. I can handle it." he replied.

After a lengthy discussion, he adamantly refused inpatient rehab, he refused Alcoholics Anonymous, and he refused individual counseling. His marriage had collapsed after years of turmoil relating to alcoholism. He hardly knew his children anymore and was behind on child support.

After a pause, which seemed frozen, I literally spoke in blunt terms: "Quit drinking or you will die and it will be soon."

Mark seem jolted into a different type of reality at this point.

"OK, OK. I know you're trying to help me." he said.

I said to him, "You have to quit and you have to start eating regular meals and get a good overall nutrition every day. I'm also going to start you on some B vitamins with thiamin and also I would like you to take a substance that you will have to pick up at the health food store. It's made from the milk thistle plant called Sylbrum. It has been shown from recent German studies that it might help protect your liver. I'd also like you to do that and then you've got to get in to your alcohol counselor."

He left somewhat in a sad daze. He showed remorse over his loss of contact with his family, and he worried about his teenage sons and whether they were using drugs and alcohol. He was very angry, but a sense of helplessness could be seen in that anger.

As I watched him lease, I realized it was a wonder that Mark was still alive and had not become another statistic. Worse yet, he could have created many other statistics out on the highway of death. I also wondered if he had been abusive to his ex-wife or children when he had been drinking prior to the divorce. I found it hard to find sympathy for him until he broke through the barrier. He really was interested in living.

Two months had passed after several visits.

"Mark, good to see you. You look better." I implied.

"Feeling a little better. Stomach has been real good." he said.

"Your last liver enzyme tests were back to normal. That is good news, Mark. But you really cannot drink again." I said.

"Haven't gone near it since I was here last." he said.

"What about A.A.A." I asked.

"Don't think the Automobile Club would want me yet but I have been making it to 2 or 3 AA meetings weekly." he chuckled.

"That's great. I better stop stuttering my vowels." I returned as I was glad to see his spirits up.

"Mark, do you see much of your sons?" I asked.

"Yes, almost every weekend for the past month. We have been having some good times. I've actually gone to Church with them and the ex once." he said.

"No kidding." I said astonished.

"You're right. I had to admit my alcoholism. I have been doing it since I was 16. My father and brothers all drank and never got treatment. The old man died in his early 50's and I was headed there too. I'm not ready for that." he concluded.

"It's a long road, Mark. Remember, that you have to stick with it." I said.

"You don't have to tell me that. Thanks for being there." he said as we shook I noticed how the whites of his eyes were clear. It was evident his jaundice days were over. A different person had left this day. His stomach pains were gone. I wondered if that ache had not been really the pain within his soul. He had healed himself and maybe helped some other lives in his journey.

Quite a Headache

◆

The lights in the exam room were off. Fran was holding a cool compress over her head suffering from a severe migraine.

"I'm not doing so well, Doc. I've been up most of the night. The migraines have come back. I've taken about a dozen Fiorinol from my other doctor's prescription. It's about a year old." Fran softly spoke.

"How long has the headache lasted?" I asked.

"Close to ten hours. It started with an unusual visual wave-like feeling. Then it hit me like a ton of bricks. I've thrown up a few times. Can you do something, Doc?

"Have you taken any other medicines except Fiorenal. No other prescriptions or any other over-the-counter drugs?" I asked.

"No." She stated.

"Your vital signs are stable and I'd like to give you a shot of a drug called Immitrex. Hopefully, it will help." I said.

Ten minutes had passed and Fran was sitting up and looked a little more settled.

"I'm doing better. Thanks, Doc." she said.

"Fran, you will need a prescription for Imimtrex if you are having a lot of severe migraine attacks and you can administer these yourself." I said.

"Thanks, Doc. That would be great. Hopefully, I'll get to work today." she said.

"Get to work? You haven't slept and you've had this terrific migraine. Go home and get some rest." I said.

"Can't do it, Doc. I'm late on a project at work and there will be hell to pay if I'm not in today." she said.

"They're really running you ragged at work, aren't they? How much sleep are you getting anyway?" I asked.

"On a good night, maybe 4 1/2 hours. I've got to leave for work at 6 a.m. It takes 1 1/2 hours to get to work 60 miles away and I'm usually not home until 8 p.m., then a few hours on the computer, squeeze in a few minutes of dinner and time with the kids and I'm out about midnight. With one in college and one two years away from college, Jerry and I both need to burn the candle to make ends meet." she sighed and continued, "Work has downsized my division and now I'm doing the work of three people it seems. No one seems to care anymore. They only tell you when you screw up. It gets pretty disheartening sometimes. I pulled an allnighter to get the project finished. Drank tons of coffee the night before and the next night was when my whopper migraine hit."

"Small wonder." I said. "Sleep deprived, corporate stress burnout and caffeine overload wth a withdrawal triggering a migraine. Fran is this worth it?"

"I can make it work, Doc. I have to. I like what I do, just a few personality conflicts lately at work." she said.

"It's making you sick, Fran. It's time to consider a better way to cope with the stress your under." I said.

"We moved out here to the country to relieve some of that stress on our family." she said, "The longer commute is still worth it, but you're right about corporate burn-out. The company is doing it to everyone. It seems fear rules along with quarterly profits."

"OK, Fran, remember the importance of sleep, stress reduction and no excess overload of caffeine and avoidance of triggers such as alcohol, cheese and MSG." I said.

As Fran was handed a list of prevention for migraines she said, "Right Doc, and thanks for fitting me in." she said as she rushed out for work.

A dose of intramuscular Imitrex gave dramatic relief of her headache. She hadn't slept and needed to get to work, a 60-mile commute.

She and her husband had decided to move to the country to raise their children in a small-town environment, in a school district safe from the problems they were seeing in the large urban school district they had come from, in a community where little leagues and local clubs established long-lasting friendships.

Fran was willing to spend more time commuting to work to have this quality of life for her family.

Now, this usually meticulously dressed, well-groomed person seemed physically let down. Her hair was completely out of place; lines of stress were obvious around her eyes.

She seemed so tired and near tears. Her migraines were getting worse, and this new medication, started today, worked wonders to give her symptomatic relief. She would learn to administer this medication at home. But that was only the beginning in helping cure her from her headaches.

She had begun to climb the corporate ladder in a Fortune 500 corporation. She was balancing the enormous time commitment and travel as a regional manager, with family life including three teenagers. The stressors of the job were beginning to wear on her. She loved that type of work, but hinted that a few of her superiors seemed to be treating her as a target of harassment. With extensive corporate downsizing, her workload seemed to have tripled.

Over the pat year, she had truly been clinically depressed and had increasing symptoms of migraine headaches and muscle tension headaches. She thought about looking for other work, but then thought about the cost of college tuition for her children. It was fast approaching.

Her symptoms had been reduced with the help of individual counseling, Prozac, migraine-prevention treatment, and oral imitrex for her migraine attacks. She revealed to me how many of her co-workers were also in counseling and on medications for depression. Many were requesting these drugs (Prozac and other SSRIs) because they enhance productivity since their workload had begun to make them feel stressed out.

Fran was approaching corporate burnout. She was a classic example of corporate downsizing. The ones remaining take on more and more work, often times in a rather inhumane way with corporations sometimes indifferent to overall mental health. What was once thought to be an American dream—climbing the corporate ladder—has now become a path to personal burnout and, often, physical deterioration. It happens all too often today.

I pondered her dilemma of trying to save for college, paying the mortgage and taxes takes two parents' incomes. Add this work stress and one can begin to see the toll on family life.

Nearly a year had passed.

Fran came in early this Winter morning. A January thaw had left a significant flooding in a nearby fields. The rain was unseasonably harsh this time of year. She was drenched and I couldn't tell if some tears had been wiped away as I entered the room.

"Well, Doc, I'm doing better with the migraines and I'm off the antidepressants, taking more vitamins, eating better, exercising and getting more rest but I'm having a big problem at work." Fran said.

I listened quietly, as she continued, "I've been getting palpitations and panic attacks when I'm at sales rep sessions. I'm one of the few female sales reps there and I've been promoted several times but I'm constantly being harassed by more than a number of my male counterparts who sometimes rudely and openly ask me to have open sex with them in very graphic terms. Sometimes in front of other men, sometimes right before I make a presentation just to give me a hard time."

I looked at her sort of stunned hardly believing that that is still going on today.

"Fran, that is blatant sexual harassment. These morons should know that, especially in the '90's. Are you the only one at work that this is happening to?" I asked.

"No. A few other women are too afraid to speak up for fear that they'll lose their jobs or be demoted or shipped off to some other place." Fran said.

"I'm documenting everything." I said, "Sounds like you need some others to help you corroborate your situation."

"You're right. I can't get anywhere with my superior who would tell me to live with it by ignoring it. He's a man and he doesn't know how degrading that is. I've talked to a few lawyers but the first two male lawyers I asked told me that it was part of the game, babe." Fran said.

The Game, I thought and then said, "What kind of idiots are out there in the corporate sale forces."

Fran responded, "More than I could ever believe, Doc."

"This is quite a headache you have, Fran." I said.

"Not as bad as the migraines, Doc." Fran said. "I'm going to take those bastards on. I think I'll tape record their comments. I think I'll find a tough female lawyer."

"Sounds good to me, Fran." I said.

Fran continued, "I'm making great money, great benefits and that's why I'm hanging in there to help pay for college for my three kids. But, you were right, life is too short for this kind of crap."

"I'm glad you're standing up to them and whether if you stay with the company or if you leave." I said.

"Believe me, I'm ready to leave and start my own business." she said.

"Go for it and good luck." I said, "I think you would be better off without medications to suppress your anxiety. I think you're better off resolving it the way you want to."

"I guess I know that but I guess I needed to hear it from you. Thanks a lot." Fran responded.

"Fran, you deserve better. Especially with your skills and attitude to be working on your own or for a business who treats you with respect. I hope you find that. I know you will." I said.

I wondered about all those folks laboring for those corporations who don't seem to care wake up every day and ask themselves, "Is it really worth it? Is it worth the sleepless nights, the irritability, the depression, the family stress?" For some of these folks, the courage to change may be the best thing that ever happened to them.

Doc, Have You Ever Smoked?

◆

Opening the door, I saw Paul sitting in his wheel chair with his nasal oxygen canula delivering continuous oxygen to his extremely emphysemic lungs. He had retired early from his factory job and had begun to slow down after he noticed that the least little bit of exertion caused profound weakness and shortness of breath. His pulmonary function was less that 20 percent of what it should have been for his age.

Paul had started smoking when he was 14 years old and continued for the next 40 years at two packs a day. Sitting, he was leaning forward, finding it easier to breath. His finger nails were yellow stained from years of tobacco use, his complexion, ashen.

He was shaking his head in an ashamed way. With the demeanor of a frightened school boy, he replied, "Don't yell at me anymore about my smoking. I'm mean as hell, so you go easy today."

Today, though, was odd because he had a peculiar rash around his face, nose, and lips.

"You're always a little mean, Paul. If you weren't, I'd think something else would be seriously wrong." I continued, "Paul, what's with the rash on your face?" as I switched gears.

"Don't ask, Doc. I'm pretty embarrassed about it." Paul rebutted and continued, "Hell, I've tried the gum, tried the patch, tried hypnosis, tried acupuncture to my ear, even tried giving up sex for awhile. Nah, just kidding on that last subject, Doc. But nothing has worked. Look at me, I need the oxygen to breathe and had to draw disability at 56 all on account of smoking cigarettes. I guess I'm weak. Others can kick it and walk away from it." he sighed

"Nicotine is a powerfully addictive drug. In some ways more addictive to some than to others." I responded.

"You're saying I'm a drug addict, Doc." he said.

"What do you think, Paul?" I asked.

"I a damned addict." he said to himself.

"Addictions can be overcome." I said.

"Well, I overcame mine two weeks ago, Doc." Paul said.

"Glad to hear it Paul. How did you do it?" I asked.

"Lit up a cigarette with my oxygen on and nearly blew up my trailer and the Mrs. to kingdom come. Should have seen it. You should have seen me, I looked like a frickin' fire breathin' dragon. I guess forgot it was on." he said.

"Paul, did you go to the Emergency Room?" I asked.

"Naw, just dunked my head in a pail of ice water and seriously thought about drowning myself for a few seconds. Too embarrassed to go to a hospital. Hell, I didn't want to come today. Guess I needed you'd be bitchin' me out. Never going to touch those god damn things again. I'm going to make sure none of my kids or grandkids are gonna keep smoking. You know how I scare the hell out of them over it?" he asked.

"How? I asked.

"Oh, I just take off my oxygen for a few minutes and they watch me turn blue. It scares the living hell out them. Doc, it's too late for me, but not too late for them. If that's one thing I can leave them with to make their lives better then, I guess, it's not all in vain." he said.

"Paul, don't give up yet. Give yourself some time to recover off tobacco. Stay in a smoke-free environment. Lot's of Vitamin C and betacarotene daily along with some Vitamin E and selenium to take daily. Maybe a little residual lung function can improve. All is not lost for you. Maybe being a human torch was a blessing in disguise for you Paul. Hopefully, things will work out." I said.

He shook his head and said, "Thanks. Hey Doc, have you ever smoked?"

I looked back at him and said, "Yeah, foolishly back in my 20's I did for awhile. Thank God, I quit."

"Good for you, Doc." he replied.

He stated that he had been still smoking a few cigarettes a day but forgot all about the oxygen being on when he decided to light up last week. He had almost blown himself up! He had burned his face, his nasal hairs and the posterior portion of his throat and nasal pharynx.

He had tried several times to quit. This time he finally did quit. It took something this severe for him to break his lifelong addiction.

Getting back to his question: Yes, I did smoke cigarettes while I was in my late twenties. I started with a few, then went up to five to ten cigarettes a day. An "occasional" became a "regular." It was when a regular became near a habit that I decided this was crazy and an absolute contradiction to what I was trying to do with my life. So it was time to quit, thank God.

A few minutes later, I looked out my window after I had talked with Paul and he had left the office. High School was out and some kids were at the edge of my parking lot smoking cigarettes. I was about ready to run out the door and yell and shoo them off the property when I saw a car pull up next to the kids. Surprisingly, it was Paul. He was driving and he stopped to talk to them. It looked as though he began lecturing them with his oxygen in place. It looked as though he was taking off his oxygen to impress his soon pale blue complexion upon them. I wish anything I could have heard what it was he was saying. I knew he was on crusade. Maybe that day he may have gotten to one of those kids. Maybe that one teenager may not develop emphysema or lung cancer or heart disease 30 years from now because Paul talked to him. Perhaps he could stop one young person from the thousands of chemicals and toxins that would poison his body throughout his life. I thought, "That a boy, Paul."

Well, Paul will be on oxygen therapy and nebulizers for his bronchial passages as long as he lives. But he has shown some promising signs of feeling a little better with more energy since he quit. He almost seemed spiritually renewed in a sense, but accepting of the fact that he had done this to his body. So he must live with the consequences. He preaches to all his family members and friends and to whomever he sees to stop and break the addiction that will eventually destroy lives.

One Meal a Day?

———————— ◆ ————————

The scale had tipped towards 250 pounds. Nancy grimaced. Her blood pressure had risen and her blood glucose was elevated. Since her last child was born, five years ago, she had continued to gain weight. She was 40 years old and 100 pounds overweight. She quietly sat on the exam table. The exam gown was fitting her quite tightly.

"Nancy, your GYN exam was OK today and it's probably time for your first mammogram." I said.

"Doc, my periods have been a lot heavier recently, especially since I put this weight on." she said.

"That can happen." I responded. "If it worsens or you become anemic from it, it might be worthwhile to get a gynecologist's opinion." I continued, "Your blood pressure is 150/95 and your blood sugar was 160 fasting and this was normal two years ago, but your weight is up 30 more pounds."

"I have sugar? Do I have to take Insulin? Am I going to lose a leg? she asked nervously.

"You have adult onset diabetes. A condition resulting often from being overweight. Your body actually produces too much insulin but your body becomes resistant to the effect of insulin which is to help uptake of blood glucose or sugar into your body's storage tissue which is your body fat or adipose tissue. Insulin resistance also may play a role in high blood pressure and disease of the arteries known as arteriosclerosis often affecting the eyes and the kidneys and small arteries and often affecting the coronary circulation and circulation to your legs if it continues not to be controlled well." I stated.

"Can drugs help this, Doc?" Nancy asked.

"Not as much as losing weight in a controlled manner. That is your best medicine." I answered.

Nancy sighed, "I weighed 140 pounds when I was married. I'd love to get back there. I'd love to start working again. I'm a good typist. I've been cooking for 4 kids and my husband, who can eat anything in sight and not gain weight. He likes dinner on the table after work. Lately, he hasn't paid much attention to me and we're getting kind of distant." she said sadly, near tears. She continued, "Growing up on a farm it seems like we ate three huge meals a day, but I didn't start gaining until I started carrying my children. I was always told, 'you gotta eat for two', and I just felt like it and didn't think much of it. But now I don't get. I only eat one meal a day. At night, we have big meal."

"How big?" I asked.

"Oh, you know, meat, potatoes, gravy, of course, vegetables, milk and dessert usually before bed." she answered.

"Do you eat any breakfast?" I asked.

"No. Guess not. Maybe snack a little when fixing the kids lunch." she said.

"Drink much fluids?" I asked.

"Pepsi." she said.

"Regular?" I asked.

"Yep. Three to four big ones a day." she replied.

"Any other little sins? How about sweets, any cravings?" I asked.

"I do crave chocolate." she replied.

"Nancy, think about what you've just told me and all the calories you consume during the day and the evening." I continued, "How about exercise?"

"Oh, I get plenty chasing after the kids." she said

"Do you walk or bike or got to exercise class?" I asked.

"Who's got time, Doc. How about those new diet pills I heard about?" she asked.

"With your blood pressure up and blood sugar elevated, I believe you're going to have to make some changes in you life. You can't continue at this pace or your health will begin to deteriorate. How old are those kids of yours?" I asked.

"Fourteen, eleven, nine and five." she replied and nodded.

In her eyes, I saw a sense of sadness and then anger at herself for letting it get his way.

"I'll try, Doc. I promise." she said.

"Great. Let's get you hooked up with a good nutritionist. Plan out some reasonable physical exercise program and start monitoring your blood pressure and blood sugar at home. It's your best feedback to help you get better. Let's try all this before we consider any diet pills. I'm not sold on them yet and they do have their side effects." I said.

She nodded, "OK. Let's get to work." It happened slowly. She gained five to ten pounds a year with surges in weight after carrying her four babies. She was attempting to return to the workplace. Numerous attempts with crash diets and mail-order gimmicks brought temporary results.

Being overweight in this rural area seems to be perceived by many as a sign of robustness and strength. Food is also a major part of the social interchanges among people in these townships; eating is a bigger part of this social interchange than it is in other places.

Her life had begun to revolve around food: it had become her security blanket.

She wanted me to so something and requested diet pills. She stated she only ate one meal a day. She appeared quite down and admitted to the daily frustration of raising children and marital stress. Her husband was becoming more and more distant physically and she feared they would separate. She ate to alleviate her stress.

After questioning further, she admitted to binge eating and often consuming snacks and food without even considering it eating. It seemed to be her drug or fix to deal with the world.

She stated she had struggled with weight since she was a teenager. Now her health was in jeopardy. She was informed of the devastating consequences of adult onset diabetes and high blood pressure with regard to long-term damage to her kidneys, her eyes, and her cardiovascular system.

She now had to come to grips with her eating habits from a behavioral standpoint in order to save her health. A nutritional counselor helped immensely with positive feedback and educational training in the proper diet.

Nancy returned for a visit. A year had nearly passed.

"Hi, Doc. What do you think?" Nancy stated as she did a complete turn around with what appeared to be a whole new wardrobe.

I was astonished. She looked like a different person; about 80 pounds lighter.

"Nancy, you look great! What was your secret?" I said.

"It was no secret, Doc. Once I left here I bought a Glucometer and checked in with a Nutritionist. Doc, I started shopping for food differently. My family noticed real soon. I turned off the television set and gave myself one hour each day to exercise. I started walking and walking and walking and then I started jogging and then I started aerobics three times a week with jogging. Then, I started lifting weights and toning. I could not believe the energy. Then, I switched from soda to water. My husband comes home and sometimes his feast isn't on the table. Too bad, huh? It's about time he learned to cook and so he has and enjoys it too, Doc." Nancy said.

I continued, after an exam, "Nancy, your blood pressure and blood sugar really have been great according to your home monitoring chart."

"Doc, I saw what happened to my aunt and my grandmother. They got heavy and developed diabetes and strokes in their 60's. Uh uh, that's not going to happen to me." she continued, "Guess what, Doc, sex life has gotten much better lately, too. I think I'm wearing my hubby out."

I laughed.

She continued, "Sometimes I go to outings and all the people want to do is eat. I'm kind of like an ex-smoker except my tobacco is fatty food. I can't believe the way I ate and let myself get that way."

I nodded in agreement and said, "Boy, I wish you could help some other folks get going."

"Doc, it's all up here." she said as she pointed to her head. "People fall into ruts and just don't get out of them until they finally see themselves in a different light. Sometimes it takes the help of others. Doc, I know I'll have to work twice as hard all my life than other people to keep the weight off. Thanks for letting me know how serious the problem was that I had."

I smiled and thought that C. Everett Koop would be so proud.

Nancy had become an exercise and diet club leader and soon helped others overcome their weight problems. I thought, "It's all in motivation in helping turn a switch on inside an individual to enact a change; whether it is eating, tobacco, alcohol or drug abuse. If that was one thing that was not taught well in Medical School, that was it. It still remains the most single challenging obstacle I face every day. To enact change in an other person's behavior.

What Am I Good for Anymore?

◆

Leona was sitting, her head resting on her cane. Her cousin—her closest of kin—met me at the door. Leona was weakened from a recent viral illness. At 93, she remained stubbornly independent.

But now her health was beginning to fade and apparently her home was, too. Her neighbors and relatives called and said it was an accident waiting to happen, and a house call confirmed this.

Once described as a meticulous housekeeper, her house looked like a bomb had hit. Papers were stacked everywhere. The kitchen was a clutter of plates and food and objects were waiting to be tripped over with an inevitable fractured hip waiting. Leona sat in what appeared to be her favorite chair. Appearing a bit down, weakened from her recent respiratory illness. Photographs and memories of decades gone by were staggered on her walls.

"How are you, Leona?" I asked.

"Been better, Doc. This damned bug has really dragged me down and it's been harder to get around. Can't see too well. Got to get my cataracts done." she said.

After examining her, she appeared to be a bit dehydrated. Her pacemaker was functioning well but she seemed to be generally weak.

"Ya know, Doc, most of my friends have gone to their maker. It seems like the only two friends that come around anymore are Ann and Arthur. Ya know what I mean?" she asked.

I shook my head "no".

Leona replied, "Ann-Gina (angina) and Arthur-Itis." she chuckled. "Well, Ann hasn't been around much since you talked me into that pacemaker and put me on that heart medicine. But, Arthur, Chrimus he comes around like bad weather and well, you know how much bad weather we have here." she said.

I nodded "yes".

"How are those boys of yours. Jonathan must be close to 6 and Ben must be almost 2. You just had a birthday and how's your wife doing?" she asked.

"Thanks for remembering and asking, Leona." I said. Wondering about her remarkable memory at 92.

Knowing that she was a staunch Republican, I asked if she was going to get out and vote in the next week's 1996 Presidential election.

"If the good Lord wills it, I'll pull those levers. You know that Bob Dole is a fine young man. He'd make a great President. He's not too old. Hell, I'm old. That Clinton, good Lord. Didn't inhale, horseshit! You are probably voting for him, aren't you Doc?" she said.

I laughed and said, "Probably."

"Leona, do you think it might be better for your health if you went to a home where people could help you with your meals and medications and daily living. I've got a place ready for you if its possible. I'm afraid if you stay here, you'll be destined to end up in the hospital either with an injury or worsening lung infection." I said.

"Bad hips, bad ticker, going deaf and need my cataracts done. Good heaven," she shook her head, "Why does the good Lord still have me around and what in tarnation am I good for anymore in this used up old body?"

"Leona," I said, "you still always make my day a little brighter."

She grinned and said, "Either you're the kindest man I've ever known or one of the biggest BSers."

We both shared a laugh.

It was painfully obvious that this woman still of sharp mind could no longer care for herself. Here was a woman who always knew the political topics of the day, sent me a birthday card every year on the exact same day, always inquired about my children, and knew their ages and names.

She was from an era that many of us no longer remember and a woman from rural America who was never afraid to tell it like it was.

Leona agreed to go to a proprietary care home. Her independence had been surrendered. She took it all in stride.

Leona, like millions of other elderly Americans, will hold onto their independence and integrity as long as humanly possible, sometimes much to the chagrin of their loved ones.

Leona moved stubbornly into her new proprietary home. A private home where a couple looked after her and four other folks that had to leave their homes for similar reasons.

"Hi Leona, how are you feeling?" I asked after Leona returned in for a check-up.

"Fine, I guess." she said.

"Is something the matter?" I asked.

"Yeah, that place you sent me to. Most of those folks all they do is complain, complain, complain. Chrimus, no one knows how to laugh over there much so I thought I'd mix it up a little over there. I've seen livelier places at cemeteries." she chuckled. "Our gal running the place has been down in the dumps, Doc, lately."

"I bet you're doing something about that, aren't you, Leona?" I said.

"I'm working on it, Doc. She's been laughing more. It is important to laugh, Doc. I don't know how I would have made it 93 years without it." she said.

"See, I told you you'd make my day. I bet you're making a few other people's days also." I said. "So, I guess that answers your question."

"What questions, Doc?" she asked.

"The question you asked to God before you went to your new home."
I replied.

"Oh, you are a charmer." she said grinning and winked.

Well, Leona's health improved at her new residence. Her caretakers have seen to her general nutrition and medication compliance. In return, she gave a great gift back to them, her shining wisdom of 93 years young. She still had a lot to give and apparently wasn't "used up" any longer. I wasn't BSing her.

Couldn't Put the Magazine Down

———————◆———————

Mary was in for her routine cholesterol and blood pressure check. She was in her usual position, sitting on the exam table, reading a magazine, her eyes hardly making contact with mine. She had always done this with her six-month visits.

I had sensed that her eyes never were truly moving along the pages. I finally asked her to do a little vision test and read a certain line. She quickly put the magazine down and said she needed glasses. Her arms suddenly crossed, as she was extremely defensive, and barked back at me, "I'm just here to get my blood pressure medicine."

"My eyes are fine, Doc." Mary snapped.

"OK, Mary." I said, holding my hands up.

"How's the article your reading in Time? I wanted to read it but ran out of time." I said as a joke.

"OK, I guess it looks like a bunch of scientists doing farm research," Mary saw, "Oh you made a joke Doc."

"What was the title of the article, Mary?" I asked.

"Beats me. I was checking out the pictures." She said.

"Mary, your blood pressure is a little high so I would like to add another medication and a potassium supplement. I'll write down instructions for you. OK?" I said.

"OK. Just give them to my pharmacist. He'll help me out." Mary said.

"Mary." I said.

"Yes, Doc." she said.

"Can you read?" I asked.

"Of course I can, Doc. I can read. Why do you ask? she said.

"Oh, Mary, I was just watching the way you were looking at the magazine and I wondered about whether you had problems with reading." I said.

"I don't have any problems. I get by OK." she said.

"Do you mind reading that print on the page there to make sure your eyes are focusing OK." I said as I pointed to a simple 4-line sentence on the title page of the magazine. Mary couldn't read it.

Mary responded, "Why do you want to know. I don't need to do this for you."

"Mary, it's OK. I just needed to know if you could read or not because sometimes there might be problems when I write prescriptions or give you things in writing and I'm not even sure that you're reading it." I said.

Mary stayed frozen, solemn and said, "Doc, I can't read. I never could read. I'm embarrassed about it and ashamed. I guess I've just tried to hide it from you and other people."

"Mary, I didn't know and I apologize if I embarrassed you." I said.

"Oh, it's all right, Doc. I know you're a nice man. Doc, I guess, back then when I was in school, I never got the help I needed. Everybody thought I was retard. Now I'm a welfare case. I don't drive a car because I can never pass the written test and not jobs nearby to do because I can't read." she said.

"Mary, there are agencies that may be able to help you and possibly help you to learn to read. Here are some phone numbers and, I believe you could take the volunteer van into the city to attend adult literacy training. We have come a long way in understanding the problem of reading disabilities." I said.

"And I thought I was getting my blood pressure checked." Mary responded. She agreed to give a try.

The reality of it was that Mary couldn't read. She was 50 years old and functionally illiterate but too embarrassed to admit it to her doctor. She had had minor labor jobs but presently was not working and was on welfare. Mary couldn't be trained for much labor and did not have a driver's license.

I finally asked if she could understand her medication directions and she said yes, but embarrassed she said that she never was able to read well. It appeared she was in special education in high school. This was back in the time when learning and reading disabilities were not well understood.

It is a significant dilemma in rural America. Illiteracy leads to inevitable poverty and often presents problems in functioning in a world where information is paramount to daily living. Understanding instructions on medications often takes a third party to intervene at home.

I tried to imagine life without being able to read. A life that leads to inevitable poverty. Not understanding basic instructions, being able to read the daily newspaper or following road signs. Never able to engage in the joy of reading a story to a child. I wondered how many were deprived of this, which to many of us seems a natural right.

Mary's triumph was to admit her problem to me and learn to turn embarrassment and adversity into learning to deal with her illiteracy. She began adult literacy training. Hopefully, her willingness to change will make her world a little better.

Humor Me

◆

The snows of December were heavy this day.

"Hey good looking!" With that familiar chuckle, this had to be one of my favorite patients. Leon was in his mid-fifties, and after two herniated discs in his lumbar spine, from a work-related injury, he since has had to cease his well-paying trucking job.

I scolded him for shoveling my office walk and asked how much he wanted to be paid.

"Nothing, just a free visit."

I replied, "Well, I can't cover you under my health insurance or my workers' compensation if you get a heart attack or your back gets worse from shoveling." We shared a laugh.

"Well, Leon, are you ready for today's procedure?" I asked.

"I've been loose as a goose for two days thanks to that frickin' dynamite colon blaster you prescribed. Now, tell me again why I need this colon scooper test." he said.

"That's a sigmoidoscopy, Leon. Because your brother and mother had a history of colon cancer and you are at risk and this lets me take a look for any lesions or polyps, and," I continued, "I hope you can lay on this table after you shoveled my walk with your back problem."

"It's OK, Doc. My back's OK since you told me to take that flax seed oil capsules, they've been helping the arthritis pain in the back. Just didn't want this little old gal behind me to fracture her hip and have her family sue you so you owe me a big one, Doc." he said.

With my helpful nurse present, we began the exam. Starting first with a digital exam prior to inserting the scope rectally.

"Jesus," Leon yelped, "I sure hope that was your finger back there."

My nurse turned ten shades of red.

"Very funny, Leon." I said and continued.

"Now comes the scope insertion. We will also be introducing a little air as I advance the scope. Any more smart ass remarks, Leon?" I asked.

As I inserted the scope.

"Christ!!! How far are you going with that thing. You probably should see my gray matter soon. You know my wife said I had shit for brains and she might be right." Leon howled.

I was having trouble focusing at this point, because I was laughing so hard.

"You got that light on now, Doc?" Leon asked.

"Yes, I do Leon and everything, so far, looks good." I replied.

"Thanks, Doc. Know something, Doc." Leon said.

"What, Leon?" I asked.

"Right now, I'm probably the brightest asshole in the whole county." he said.

"Did you spell whole beginning with "W" or an "H"?" I asked.

Leon couldn't hold it any longer and his long windiness ended with resounding breaking of wind. Thank God for gown's and goggles.

"Well, Leon, you made it and your colon is nice and clean and no evidence of any problems." I said.

"Thanks, Doc. Let's not do this real soon again. OK?" Leon said.

Turning to his general health, I said, "Well, how's the rest of you. Did you quit smoking?" I asked.

"I'm better, Doc. The medicine you and the heart doc gave me have helped my chest pain and nerves and that lady counselor has been helping and nno-oo I haven't quit smoking." Leon said.

"Leon, you know the score since your by-pass surgery. You have to stop or you run a risk of having your grafts plug up again and Leon that is not compatible with life and also smoking is not helpful to those with deteriorating disc disorders." I said.

"Jesus, you really are giving me the inside out job today and after I shoveled your walk." Leon said.

"Wouldn't be doing my job if I didn't say that, Leon." I replied.

"I know Doc and I appreciate your honesty but life's been a little rough since the back has put me out on disability and can't even earn the same amount of money as before. I also have a couple young teenage grandchildren my wife and I have custody of. Sometimes, I could take up drinking too. But, hell, they need a solid home and they've got one. Just a lot of stress and I guess the cigs are a crutch. I'll quit someday." Leon said.

"You doing a little mechanic work." I said.

"Yeah, small engine, but most of the folks are short of cash so I sometimes fix a lot of stuff for nothing." Leon said.

"You're a good guy, Leon." I said.

"Hey, gotta try." Leon said as he winked.

"Been getting Disability for my back and heart disorder. I feel kind of guilty, I guess, but I'm 55-years old and who is going to hire me now?" Leon said.

"Do you get any more anginal pains since the bypass?" I asked.

"Yeah, Doc. Mostly when I'm directing traffic at fires and car accidents for the Fire Department." Leon answered.

"What else are you doing besides doing auto repair and working for the Fire Department?" I asked.

"Well, I do crossing guard at the school a couple a days a week. I volunteer for that but I don't get any chest pain there, Doc. I feel bad having to be on SSI Disability. I just want to somehow give something back to my community. It seems everybody looks on anyone who gets a government subsidy as some sort of panhandler. I don't want to be in that position but I don't known how we would survive since my disc injury and heart attack. I guess there may be some people out there that take advantage of that situation. I'm not one of them, Doc and I feel bad about that. I've always pulled my own weight up until the last couple of years." Leon said.

"Well, it sounds like your still carrying yours and many others also, Leon." I replied.

Here was a guy who would give the last dime he had if a stranger needed to make a phone call.

His ability to laugh was vital to his recovery, but it wasn't always that easy for him.

The stress of losing his job, excessive tobacco smoking, poor diet, and chronic back pain had led to significant depression and to coronary artery disease. He had recently undergone quadruple bypass surgery, but still was battling cigarette use and overcoming his depression through counseling and medication. He worked part time, often doing small-engine repair, but many times he did his work for free. He liked to help others out, sometimes at the expense of himself. He was raising his grandchildren, who were in their early teens after their parents had split up and left the state.

Leon, like hundreds of thousands of others who are injured in the workplace, or disabled from other accidents, so knows how his life changes.

Leon adapted to his adversity and continues to try to help his neighbor, family, and friends with his persistent positive outlook. He has worked through his disability and has not given up. He grew from these adversities.

Here was a man for whom everything in his life seemed to add up to adversity, yet he persevered through a faith in life itself. He kept a sense of humor and always brought laughter to our office. It often was his therapy for his chronic back pain and his ailing heart.

Do You Think I Have A Problem?

◆

Dave's wife, Linda stopped by the office before she left for her morning job.

"Hi, Doc. Dave would kill me if I was here so please don't tell him." Linda said.

"What can I do for you, Linda." I asked.

"Doc, Dave's coming in for a problem with a cough but I wish you would give him a good going over." she said.

She continued, "Doc, he's not eating much and losing weight. I've been reading up on bipolar disease. I think he has it. Sometimes, he is so irritable and mean and sometimes he is so up with lots of energy. Lately, though, he's been a real SOB and very self-centered in his actions. Doc, our marriage is on the rocks. I can't be the only one working. He's just drifting between jobs. Our daughter will be starting college next year and she's really worried, too. He's like a different person from the one I married 18 years ago. We're both 40 and I want to make this marriage last but something is seriously wrong with him. He still drinks a little and still smokes but I don't know how he is spending his days lately. He's so up and down."

"Thanks, Linda. I know you're very concerned and I know you care or you wouldn't be here." I said.

I continued, "I'll see what I can do but what transpires between Dave and I is confidential in nature as is our discussion." I said.

"I appreciate that, Doc. I hope you can help." she sighed.

Dave had a cough that wouldn't quit. He appeared quite disheveled and unkempt. He had drifted between jobs. Looking quite emaciated, I inquired how much he was smoking.

"Pack a day," he replied.

"Do you drink?" I asked.

"Oh, a little here and there."

"Do you smoke anything else, like reefer?" I continued.

"Yeah. I still partake," he honestly replied. Then he paused and asked, "How about free-basing? Does that bother your lungs?"

"Free-basing cocaine?" I asked, somewhat astonished, "Of course it will, as will pot smoking and one pack a day of cigarettes. What are you doing to yourself, and how long have you been using cocaine?"

"Over ten years, but free-basing for about a year," he answered.

"Do you think you have a drug problem," I asked.

"No, do you think I do?" Dave replied. We locked into a stare, and I quietly shook my head "yes." He understood.

I began to realize as I thought, "This guy really believed his drug use was not a problem and did not matter much. His marriage was in serious trouble, he had lost several jobs, and he daily used cocaine and alcohol. "Denial" was an understatement and his use was hidden from his spouse.

"Never looked at it as a problem. Just something I do, I guess." Dave said.

"Where are you working these days, Dave?" I asked already knowing the answer.

"Nothing lately. No work lately. The economy is kind of slow. Do a little woodcrafting here and there." Dave said.

"Do you find yourself using more cocaine when you're not working?" I asked.

"No. Sometimes I used it more when I was on some construction job. Lots of people using it, gives them a lift, I guess." Dave replied.

I shuddered at the thought of recent construction projects and having my family present in buildings where construction workers had chronically been under the influence of cocaine or other drugs.

"How's the rest of your life going, Dave?" I asked.

"What do you mean?" he replied. "OK, I guess. Wife's been real bitchy lately."

"Dave, does she know about your cocaine use?" I asked.

"Not lately. She used to smoke a little pot in the past herself but she is dead set against drugs now since we had our daughter." he replied.

"Ever thought of getting treatment?" I asked.

"You mean like junkies get for heroin?" Dave asked.

"Have you ever used needle drugs, Dave?" I asked.

"Oh, about 5 years ago." he replied. "Then, I decided, better not."

"Dave, have you ever been worried about contracting HIV, AIDS or Hepatitis?" I asked.

"Oh, believe me, I sterilized those needles." Dave said.

"Dave, would you still consider being screened for HIV, Hepatitis B and Hepatitis C?" I asked.

"Why?" he asked.

"Because you have put yourself at risk, especially 5 years ago." I said.

"No. I wouldn't want to know." Dave said.

"Dave, what about your wife and your daughter?" I asked.

"What about them?" he replied defensively.

"You may have put them at risk. If you are HIV positive or Hepatitis B or C, you could transmit the virus sexually or via drug borne transmission." I said.

"Oh. OK. It's just a blood test. Go ahead." he said.

After verbal and written form consent, Dave consented to a screen.

"Do you believe you are addicted to cocaine?" I asked.

"No, not really. I'll stop if I need to." he replied.

"Dave, cocaine is a drug that works on the dopamine pathway system in the brain. It affects the neuro chemicals involved with the fight or flight response,. The release of adrenaline into the body. I creates a sense of euphoria and invincibility. But it is only temporary. Chronic use creates a depletion of these natural neurotransmitters that results in mood swings, paranoia and delusional thinking. It can also cause some serious cardiac problems. People that overuse these drugs or even use these drugs become very self-absorbed, putting the drug and oneself at the highest priority with everyone and everything else in life becoming less important such as family, marriage, children and work. Dave, does this ring a bell?" I continued, "Dave, would you consider more intensive treatment to get yourself free from this drug."

Dave fell quiet and said, "Doc, are you going to do anything about my cough?"

"Sure, Dave. You have bronchitis. Here is a prescription for antibiotics. You need to do the rest. Also, quit smoking. We'll check a chest X-ray to make sure your lungs are OK." I said.

"I'll see you, Doc." Dave scurried out of the office in a cocky mood.

I was wondering whether he was just coming down from his last high. I wondered if I had pushed too hard. One thing for sure, he was not a manic depressive as his wife thought. He hid his drug use but not his behavior which most likely revealed some pretty bizarre mood swings. I wondered if Dave would make his change or if he would end up just another statistic, just another life ruined.

Six months had passed. Linda stopped in for a routine check-up.

"Doc, I wanted to let you know that Dave is working and has been clean for 4 months. He has to be to keep his job because they drug test him." Linda said.

"That's good news." I replied.

"I want to thank you. I suspected he was using drugs. He told me a few days after he saw you and I gave him an ultimatum: get into treatment or he was out the door. He decided treatment was better than the other place he was going." she said.

I smiled realizing that it took more than my persuasion on many occasions to help someone make that change.

Dave was one of the lucky ones. He had someone who cared and loved him enough and was willing to stand firm. He was four months free of a self-induced mental and physical illness. I only hope that the road he was now traveling was a journey into wisdom.

Set in Her Ways

◆

I was called back to the emergency room at 3 a.m. Leo had come in by ambulance in respiratory arrest. He was intubated and on a ventilator. Thelma was his wife of 50 plus years, and now she sat faithfully at his side, clutching his swollen hand.

She quietly stood as I entered. She was dressed in her old style farm dress and sweater, her hands cuffed firmly on both hips and tapping her foot. I sensed a demanding sense of urgency to quickly attend to her husband.

Reading her mind, I felt a little uneasy at first, "Who was this young whipper-snapper wet-behind-the-ears young doctor?"

"Just get up from your beauty rest?" Thelma needled me.

"Sorry, Thelma, the ER called me at 3:00 a.m. and said Leo needed admission." I said.

"Leo's not looking so good, Doc. Got him on this breathing machine and giving him all these drugs. Did you get all the information needed from the nurses, those lovely gals." she said.

"He has a respiratory infection which tipped him into respiratory failure due to a severe breathing disorder, Thelma." I said.

"You sure you can handle this, Doc? How old are you anyways?" Thelma asked.

"I forgot Thelma. How old are you? Forty-two, forty-three?" I said.

"Oh, aren't you a charmer." she said.

"I'll ask for a pulmonary specialist Thelma to see Leo but I'll be following his case daily." I reassured her.

"Thanks. Just get him better, Doc." Thelma said.

"We'll try Thelma but remember, Leo has a very severe lung disease due to chronic exposure to asbestos and also due to chronic farmer's lung disease. A condition acquired by long sensitivity to inhaled mold spores over the years. You go home and get some sleep, Thelma." I said.

"Think I'll stay here, Doc. I can sleep anywhere."

The next morning in the hospital, there was Thelma at Leo's bedside. She looked up, hands on her hips and stated, "About time you got here. What are you on banker's hours?"

It was 8:15 a.m. and I just got back to bed at 4:30 a.m.

"Hi, Thelma. How are you? Leo's holding his own overnight. So that's good news. His breathing condition is going to take a few days to get him off the ventilator, though." I said.

"What's the matter with his testicles, Doc?" she asked.

I replied, "The swelling is due to his right sided heart failure."

"His skins all broke out and none of the creams they are using are helping him. I got my homemade salve with me and I'm going to use it on him. So don't try to stop me." she said.

"I won't Thelma. I'm sure its good stuff." I said.

The next day Thelma came up to me in the hospital and said, "Well, Doc, you're all right by me. I met your wife, she took care of Leo last night. She's a fine nurse. If you're married to her, that's one plus in your favor."

"Well, thanks Thelma. I've always known that." I replied.

"How's her gardens doing and how's that boy doing?" she asked.

"Great. Thanks for asking." I said.

"You got some big dogs, too, don't ya?" She asked.

"Yes, Newfoundlands. My wife's other love also." I said.

"Oh, they're beautiful animals. We have a collie, just love her. I brought some asparagus and onions by your office. They're both very nutritious and grown without any chemicals." she said.

"Thanks, Thelma. I really appreciate that." I said.

She had been her husband's primary caretaker, and I had to be very careful in letting her know we would be partners in her husband's care.

Thelma was clearly set in her ways. She wasn't going to have it any other way.

It was the way she raised her family, kept her house, tended to her flowers, grew her vegetables, nurtured her pets, and now cared for her husband. On my previous visits, she had lectured me on the merits of onions and asparagus and had always asked how my wife's flowers were doing and how my children were.

Years of farming and factory work had resulted in a mixed respiratory problem of farmers lung (a lung disorder resulting from chronic exposure to grain feed mold spores) and asbestosis. This problem resulted in a severe restrictive lung disorder and rendering him unable to breath deeply and to properly exchange the oxygen and carbon dioxide we all take for granted each day of our lives. This disorder had rendered him quite inactive, but his appetite never quit. He had become very obese, and this made his respiratory condition much worse. Thelma loved to cook and she had waited on Leo hand and foot tirelessly for the past few years.

This was not Leo's first time in for respiratory problems. Several house calls to their trailer out in the back roads had helped ward off several potential admissions, but pulmonary infection tipped him over the edge into respiratory failure this time. He had a terminal lung disease.

Days in the intensive care passed as we attempted to cure his infection and wean him off the ventilator. He had developed severe swelling (edema) of his legs and abdomen. His scrotum had increased to the size of a grapefruit due to the right-sided heart failure from his respiratory problem. With his obesity problem and resulting hygiene dilemma, he developed a severe rash in his groin, for which multiple regimens of topical prescriptions were tried. Thelma was concerned, constantly inquiring about his rash but never about his overall condition. She finally brought in her own homemade salve, and as I rounded every morning, there she would be massaging Leo.

Well, the salve cleared up Leo's rash. I came in one morning and said, "Good work." Thelma was now concerned about an embarrassing pimple on my nose, and after two days she offered her miracle salve to clear up my nose. I thanked her but said I thought it would clear up okay.

Leo recovered to go home and Thelma, always at his side in the hospital, refused home health aides at home and again took care of her partner head to toe. She at first felt helpless, but then she became empowered in helping him recover and soothe his discomfort. She felt no loss of dignity in attending to his bodily needs and discomfort.

My last house call to them, before he passed on in his sleep, revealed her comfort and calming effect on a sometimes difficult man. This was unconditional love. They seemed to have been from a time gone by. Fifty-plus years together in hard times, together raising a family, and finally in sickness.

Thelma's health began to fail after Leo passed on. A cancer developed in her liver which took her life after she had given up the will to live on at 80 years of age. She wanted no treatment as she knew it would not cure her. Her time had come, and she accepted it gracefully. She had always been set in her ways, and she always went out of her way to remind me of that.

Fear and Loathing at the Doctors

◆

The screaming voice of a child with an equally frantic mother had emerged in my treatment room one early, warm, summer morning. I had to do a double take.

Jennifer had been fishing with her brother at the river. He had made a furious cast and had hooked Jenny right through her nasal septum. It had entered her right nostril with the barb protruding out her left nostril.

"Hold still hon, the Doctor will help you." Jenny's mom said.

"Oh, Doctor, please do something quick." Jenny's mom said and continued by addressing her son, "and you, young man, out in the waiting room. You, you're in big trouble." she said.

Jenny's brother left quite briskly.

Having to run to another room to get a topical anesthetic, a fellow was put in there, waiting for me, kind of a woodchuck type of character, very unkempt, with rather grimy clothes and a few teeth missing, hadn't shaved in a week, and he proceeded to make the comment, "That kid must be a hell of a fisherman. Couldn't a hooked a catch any better than that, wu-whee, right through the gills."

I looked in a very puzzled manner at this bizarre man, secured the necessary medical supplies and ran back to attend Jenny.

"Now, Jenny, I'm just going to clear all the stuff off the hook and then give you some medicine to take the hurt away." I said.

"Get the worm out of me. Oh—oh." she cried.

"Jenny, the Doctor is going to help you. Just hold still." her mother said.

Just then, I noticed a silence in the room. As my nurses were restraining Jenny and soothing her, Jenny's mother had suddenly gone through a rapid color change from red to pale white.

"I gotcha." I said as I caught her fainting backwards. "Rest her on the floor." I said after putting a cool compress on her forehead.

While all fell quite in my treatment room which was quite close in proximity to the waiting room, as I was letting a topical anesthetic set in to Jenny and tending to her mother, I could hear the sounds of the waiting room. Jenny's brother, Billy, had escaped out to the waiting room. He, unfortunately, had sat down next to the town's busybody couple. Mr. and Mrs. Busybody began their interrogation of Billy. I could everything quite loud because they are both a little hearing impaired as they were of a little advanced age. As they began to cross-examine him.

"What's your name, son?" Mr. Busybody asked.

"Billy." Billy replied.

"What. Speak up. Billy who?" Mrs. Busybody asked.

"Billy Newcomb." Billy replied.

"What happened to your sister?" Mr. Busybody asked.

"She got a fishhook stuck in her nose. We were on the bridge and I was casting my fishing rod and it got stuck." Billy said.

"Ah, you gotta be more careful, young man, with a rod. You fishin' for bullhead?" Mr. Busybody asked.

"Yes, at the bridge." Billy said.

"Quimby's Bridge on the river?" Mr. Busybody asked.

Billy nodded, "Uh huh."

"You folks live down there?" Mr. Busybody asked, "Nice area."

"What does your Dad do?" Mrs. Busybody asked.

"He works at the power plant." Billy answered.

"How about your Mom?" Mrs. Busybody asked.

"Home with us. She does stuff but she doesn't have to work." Billy said.

"Oh, probably can because those power plant jobs pay pretty good money, I understand." Mr. Busybody said.

Just then, another character spoke up. I knew who it was. A friendly old burn-out from the '60's. He then stated, "She's a little young for nose piercing. Don't ya think. Ha ha."

A very strange conversation was ensuing in the waiting room while I tended to Jenny and her Mom lying on the floor with a cool compress.

"You got a power boat?" Mrs. Busybody asked.

"Yes." Billy answered.

"How many horsepower." Mr. Busybody asked.

Billy shrugged, "I don't know."

"Now which house is yours?" Mr. Busybody asked.

"We live in a white house on the river lane." Bill answered.

"Oh nice, that must have cost some bucks I bet." Mr. Busybody said.

"What's your Dad do for the power company?" Mrs. Busybody asked.

Billy fell silent, thank God. I was hoping he would tell him that his father was Chairman of the Board. That really would have shut them up for awhile. Oh God, I thought. By the time their done with this kid, they'll know what his family's adjusted gross income will be, how many bathrooms they have in their house and how many times they're probably using it a day when they're finally finished interrogating Billy. I couldn't think of a punishment that Billy's mother could invent for him that was worse than what he was going through. I'll bet he'll always be more careful casting his fishing line from here on out.

Turning back to Jenny's mom as she was gradually coming to she said, "I can't believe this. I've never fainted before."

"Never seen your daughter like this before either. Lay down and relax." then I turned to Jenny and continued, "Jenny, this medicine is helping the hurt isn't it?"

She replied, "Uh-huh."

With her a little distracted by my nurse telling her about her horses, the hook was removed in a forward direction with a little cautery needed to stop any mild bleeding.

"When are you gonna start?" she asked.

"All done, Jenny. Now we'll get you, your Mom and your brother home." I said.

The hard part was not giving a local anesthetic and removing the hook but in gaining a six-year-old's trust.

"Oh, I'm so embarrassed, Doc, about my fainting here. Thanks for everything." Jenny's mom said.

"Oh, it's OK. Somethings sometimes are out of your control and that is sometimes the hardest thing to deal with especially when it's your own child. Sometimes doctor's offices create a lot of anxiety. I often see this a lot with kids. Sometimes, it often starts at an early age when they come in for shots, for minor traumas, sometimes fainting at the sight of blood often results from some fearful memory of being a kid. Many adults hate seeing a doctor themselves. Oftentimes, they put off some serious medical problems. Some of them come in with blood pressures out of control because they're scared to see the doctor and the adrenaline is flowing. I guess to many folks its just that loss of control with regards to the doctor/patient relationship."

"Well, thanks for putting Jenny at ease and thanks for helping me out." she said.

"I don't think Jen will have a problem coming in here again." I said.

Well, Jenny was a trooper. I wondered if it were my child, how I might have reacted in her mom's situation. I guess that's why my wife takes our kids to a different physician as many physicians often choose to do.

Jenny has returned many times for well visits and other brief problems. She shows no fear, but I'm not sure if she will ever fish with her brother again and I'm also not sure whether Billy will ever hang out in our waiting room again.

Keep on Truckin'

◆

A lake Ontario lake-effect storm had covered the landscape with a carpet of glistening snow on this February morning. A break from the clouds had brought brilliant sunshine.

Gazing out my office window, I noticed a doe crossing in the field across the road near one of the small lakes in this countryside rich with nature's gifts.

Suddenly, a tractor trailer pulled in front of my view across the highway, and the deer scattered. A man got out slowly and, holding his chest, he came to the front desk. My nurse picked up on his problem and whisked him into or treatment room.

His hair was completely frazzled. He looked like he had dressed in a hurry, shirt partly unbuttoned and partly tucked in, with his shoes unlaced. He looked a bit pale, a little short of breath, and very frightened.

"You the Doctor?" the fellow asked.

"Yes." I answered.

"Saw your office and stopped by rig." he said. He continued, with troubled breathing, "Doc, after I left a friend's place were I stayed last night I was ready to make my two-week run when I had the damnedest pain in my shoulder and left arm. I don't feel well."

As he spoke my nurse ran a cardiogram.

"How long has it been going on?" I asked.

"Um, about better 3/4 of an hour, but it's getting worse." he said.

He was perspiring heavily as he spoke, "Kind of hard to breathe."

"How old are you, sir?" I asked.

"Will's my name Doc." as he stuck his hand out and we shook hands, he continued, "I'm 50 years old last week."

"Well Happy Birthday." I replied and continued, "Will, have you ever been treated for a heart condition and do you smoke and are you on any medications." I asked.

"Yes, I smoke. I haven't seen a doctor in ten years. I avoid them like the plague. I'm not on any medications." he replied.

"Well, your cardiogram we're running here shows your having poor blood flow to a certain portion of your heart probably." I said.

"You mean a heart attack, Doc?" he asked.

"Possibly. We need to get you to the hospital as soon as possible. We're going to give you a nitroglycerin tablet, some oxygen and aspirin and some medicine called Lidocaine because your heart is showing a lot of irregularities. The ambulance will be coming very shortly to take within a few minutes." I said.

"Jesus, Doc, you sure?" Will asked.

"I'm sure." I replied.

Will mumbled something, "Should have left last night. Kind of over-did it this morning."

"What?" I asked.

"Oh, I'll tell you later." he answered.

Just then, his lady fried arrived very worried. Talked with Will but then jumped in his rig to take it back to her place after he asked her to and off Will went speeding to the hospital in the ambulance.

A brief history from this unknown 50-year-old man and a revealing electrocardiogram diagnosed an acute myocardial infarction—a heart attack. Oxygen and IV lidocaine (?) were administered for frequent but possibly dangerous premature ventricular beats. The local volunteer ambulance arrived, and after I discussed triage and faxed his cardio-gram to the closest emergency room—20 miles away—he was whisked away, awaiting the clot buster (T.P.A.) after prompt evaluation by a cardiologist, which prevented serious long-term damage to his heart.

Will stopped in after his hospital stay. "Hey, Doc. I wanted to thank you for your help, you know. I'm mostly on the road but I do need a regular doctor and I do get back here every couple of months to see my lady friend. In fact, Doc, that was what brought on the heart attack. We were really getting it on sort of an out the door finale and hell I thought I was a goner but didn't. After I left her, I got in my truck and felt funny, then I couldn't breathe, well, I saw your office and pulled in." Will said.

"Glad you did, Will." I said. "Will, you need to stay on one Aspirin a day and your beta blocker and here is a guide to a low-cholesterol diet and a list of some extra vitamins and supplements to take."

"Christ, you know the types of places truckers eat at. Fried grease and more fried food, add some pie and coffee, donuts." Will said.

"That has to change, Will. Your arteries cannot handle it. Your cath report after the T.P.A. was pretty good. You can manage this with the proper diet and supplement medicines and exercise." I said.

"That's what I wanted to talk to you about, Doc." Will said.

"Exercise?" I asked.

"Sort of." Will said.

"Walking is great. Do as much as you can" I said.

"That's not what I was going to ask." Will continued, "How about me and Wilbur?"

"Who's Wilbur?" I asked.

"You know, Wilbur." he said as he looked down toward his zipper.

I laughed and said, "You passed your stress test with a pretty good level of MET's which means that your heart is getting enough adequate blood supply. I think you'll be OK." I said.

"Well, I'm thankful for that, Doc, as are my lady friends." Will said.

"Friends?" I replied, thinking in a plural sense and continued, "I hope your using your condoms."

"Always, Doc, always." Will replied.

"Now, lastly, smoking. Quit now or eventually you'll have another heart attack. Whatever it takes, hypnosis, acupuncture, medication to help you, you must do it." I said.

"I can do that. I'm just glad you weren't going to take away my sex life. God forbid." Will said.

"Be careful out there, Will." I said.

"Doc, I'm going to take the next month off anyways. A little vacation out to Vegas." Will said.

I thought about all the lifestyle changes I had just talked to him about and wondered if some quiet beach would be a little better place for him, but he'd probably be happier in Vegas.

With manufacturing and agricultural jobs shrinking, Will, like many workers with only high school educations in rural America make up a sizable part of the truckers of America. Their diet is absolutely horrendous, high in fats, eating at most of the greasy spoons that dot the interstate landscape. Many of them smoke also, and the hours they keep makes one worry about the safety of the highways. Their long-term health following these life patterns becomes rather obvious.

Well, six weeks had passed and Will stopped back in.

"Well, Doc, made some changes. Still working on that smokin', down to 2-3 cigs a day but I've been changing my diet and even have a special cooler in the refrigerator. I'm takin' aspirin, my beta blocker, and my other extra antioxidants you told me about. Christ, it's hard to remember to take all those things: betacarotene, Vitamin C, folic acid, whatever and that other stuff, selenium and Vitamin E in the evening. But I'm doing it, Doc." Will said.

"Good, Will. Keep it up. Just gotta quit smoking." I replied.

"Take care, Will." I said as Will left the office.

"You too, Doc. Take care of yourself and I'll see you after the Summer is over." Will replied.

I watched as Will left the office, climbed up into his rig and headed out on the highway.

He had begun driving again and carried a special refrigerator in his tractor trailer. His cholesterol had dropped because he had totally altered is diet. He was still struggling with nicotine but was making an effort. He wanted to drive for five more years before retiring. I think he enjoyed his nomad life, a sailor in this never-ending sea of a mobile world of consumer products.

I hope he enjoys his retirement years, and I hope he gets there.

Flight of the Snow Birds

———————————— ◆ ————————————

That familiar sound of Canadian geese stopped in again to visit this region of small lakes and generous farm fields in the magnificent kaleidoscope of Central New York's autumn landscape. It was October, and it was time for another migration: the flight of the snow birds. Hundreds of senior citizens would roll in for their check up, flu shot, and winter supply of prescriptions before they headed south for the winter.

Charlie and Evelyn were in today, always tanned and, at 86 and 85 years respectively, they were remarkably spry. Since their retirement as high school teachers, they split their lives between here and Florida.

Charlie came in for a checkup and a renewal of his blood pressure and prostate medicine which, fortunately for him, was only one single pill he had to take daily.

"Now, Doctor, I want a good going over before we head South." Charlie said.

"And how's Charlie?" I said.

"You know, he never says much, so how am I to know if anything's wrong with him." Evelyn said.

"Charlie's fine." he replied.

"Ready for another great winter in sunny Florida?" I asked.

"Ha, as long as we can stay healthy, please be sure to give me a hundred days supply of medicine. I don't want to see any doctors down there." she said.

"Well, there are lots of good doctors in Florida." I said.

"Well, I haven't found one I liked. I feel like a guinea pig when I've gone to see different doctors. I'm afraid they'll try to take use off some of the medicine that's helping me and putting me on something after they run about $10,000.00 worth of tests on me. They probably only needed a $35.00 office visit. That's why I come here only and I'll call you if I get sick down there." she said.

"Well, we'll have to find someone you can go to if you need to, Evelyn." I said.

"Well, Doc, my nerves have been real bad ever since that flimflam man came by this summer and robbed the house after trying to give a phony estimate to repair the outside porch." she continued, "Marion, my neighbor, said 'Now Evelyn you've always played in the Key of High C, so you get some nerve medicine before you have a stroke'" she said.

"Well, did the Tranxene help you? I noticed your blood pressure is better and you seem a little calmer." I said.

"Now, Doctor, I don't want to become a drug addict, but 1/2 of a tablet twice a day has really helped. Charlie has even noticed it." she said.

"You won't be an addict if it's helping you and it is helping you and your blood pressure." I continued, "You take care driving South."

"Charlie does most of the driving. You know us, we're the ultimate snowbirds. Gotta fly with those geese." she said.

Evelyn, however, needed more reassurance that her health was good enough for her to go south. She would remind me that she always "played in the key of high C." Renewing her anti-anxiety medicine, I nodded and replied, "How could I ever forget that?" She felt at home with her hometown family doc but was very apprehensive about seeking extensive medical care in Florida.

"You know, Doctor, this is our home. The Winters are too long here, sometimes starting well before Thanksgiving and lasting through until Easter. Sometimes 2-3 foot of snow out there with drifts up to 5 foot in the middle of January. So, we have a much healthier life in the warm Southern climate, getting more fresh air and exercise than those who stick up here but we sure would like to be back home." he said.

I thought about Charlie and Evelyn and sometimes worried a little bit about them and encouraged not to drive for long distance periods due to their overall and hope that every Winter they would never have any problems with their advancing age on the highways.

I thought of all of those snowbirds packing up on their annual excursions, cramming the North-South Interstates in October and early November.

Charley and Evelyn returned on a day the geese, by the thousands, found temporary haven across the road from my office. Two very large folders were accompanying them as I entered the room.

"Well, Doctor, am I ever happy to see you." Evelyn said. "Charley went to the hospital after he went to the Emergency Room for dizziness. Now, look at all the tests they ran, EEG, an MRI, Holter Monitor, echocardiogram, then a cardiac catheterization which turned out pretty good. Thank goodness we have a couple layers of insurance. Look at this medical bill, the totals were close to $12,000.00. Well, they finally put him on Antivert for an inner ear disorder and he was fine after that."

"Why couldn't they have put me on this $10.00 prescription drug and said the hell with all these other tests." Charley spoke out.

"That's a good question, Charley." I replied. "I wasn't there to make the calls."

"Doctor, I got so worried about Charley that my nerves got going, my blood pressure went really high and I got dizzy. Next thing you know, I'm in the hospital getting an MRI, EEG, an echocardiogram and all sorts of X-rays and blood tests. Well, they didn't do anything so I took on extra Tranxene a day and I felt great." Eveylen said.

I started laughing with them and said, "Wish you would have called me. It's OK to when you're in Florida."

"No wonder Medicare is going broke, Doc. I feel guilty about this but we really were at the physician's mercy and they didn't know us well and probably felt they were being thorough." Evelyn said.

"Thorough" I thought to my self. I wondered how much time they actually talked one on one with Charley or Evelyn before they went ahead with their barrage of tests.

I responded, "There are many fine physicians in Florida, but I have had a suspicion that, if Medicare did an audit on health care expenditures in that state, they would find a lot of overutilization of medical resources, not always clearly needed or in the best interests of the patient."

Charley and Evelyn began to leave. I realized that the flight of the snow birds has also caused a flight of physicians, many now competing in an aggressive health care market, attempting to maximize their profits.

Charlie and Evelyn left in a good mood that morning. "Glad to be home." Evelyn said.

Charlie and Evelyn, as well as the Canada geese, always remind me when spring finally appears here. Evelyn kind of reminds me of that leader in the front of the "V" of the geese in flight with her song resonating in the key of high C.

Journey to a New Land

———————— ◆ ————————

What was all the excitement about? A moose had come next door to the elementary school. The children flocked out with their teachers in amazement. Two days later, he had found what seemed like a comfortable place in a cow pasture of a local farm family. People came from around the area to see this moose, with an impressive rack. Sometimes the farmer found it a little inconvenient.

I saw the farmer's wife, a young Mennonite woman with her two little children that were in the office for a well child exam today.

"I drove out to your farm yesterday." I said.

"Oh, did you Doctor. Did you see the moose?" she replied.

"Yes, and lots of other people and a television crew filming the moose. You should have sold tickets." I said.

"My husband's not laughing. He can't get some of his cows to come in to be milked because that moose is to close to them." she continued, "He's in love. It's mating season and he's really confused." she joked.

"Did anyone name that moose?" I asked.

"No, not yet. What do you think he should be called?" she asked.

"Well, he's got an impressive rack and he's taken to a few of your prize milking cows. Why don't we call him Horny." I said.

"That's perfect." she laughed, "My husband will love it."

"How has Carl been doing since the accident, Mary?" I asked.

"Carl's right back to work Doctor. Thanks for asking." she continued, "that artificial hand is working great. He's able to work the farm."

"Lost it in the large combine, didn't he?" I asked.

"His sleeve got caught and the shut down switch didn't work quick enough," she continued, "but he thanks the Lord that he is alive and can still provide for his family."

"He's a hard worker, as you are Mary." I said.

"We are blessed with good farm land and seven healthy children." she replied.

"Have the hospital bills been tough?" I asked.

"Our church helped. It came to over Fifty Thousand Dollars, but it's paid for." she replied.

I paused in a somber respect for these folks and gently nodded.

"Well I hope Carl can get horny away from his cows." I said.

We laughed again.

It was mating season, and this moose got quite attached to a few dairy cows. He had come hundreds of miles, from his home in the northern Adirondack mountains.

His journey changed finally when the conservation officer came with his tranquilizer gun and took him back to the mountains.

It was quite a novelty to the area. A moose had never wandered this far before. He seemed so foreign in the very familiar landscape.

What was interesting was that our journeyman moose had nestled down on a farm owned by a local Mennonite family. This family, like several dozen others of Amish stock, had also journeyed, this time from Lancaster, Pennsylvania, after less and less land was available there for agricultural use.

The Mennonite families have no doubt brought a different culture to this rural region. Hard working dairy farmers, who have rather large families of often up to eight children, who live and share among themselves. Most women have their babies via home deliveries by their own midwife. They have their own school and church, of course.

This young farmer had had an amputee accident to his hand with extraordinary hospital cost. He had no health insurance, but his bill was paid as the local and distant Amish polled their monetary resources to meet the costs.

Their clothes are home made, as is much of their food. Their children are always well dressed and respectful and quiet. The consult me appropriately for medical problems and understand common sense. Their bills are always paid. For a physician, they are often a dream come true.

There is a certain peace I sense among them, a sense of understanding their place in the world with a strong spiritual base. Sometimes I wish many of us could take a lesson from this simplicity of their living.

These families were a novelty and different at first. Their journey north has brought a new enrichment to this region.

A Past Unimaginable

———————◆———————

"Doc, moved up in the area a couple of months ago and needed a family doctor." Jerry said.

"Where are you from, Jerry?" I asked.

"Vegas. For the last 20 years I was a pit boss." Jerry responded.

"Interesting." I said.

"Got tired of it, Doc. Got married last year and settled here close to my wife's family. Vegas is no life for being married and raising a family." he said.

"Let's see. You're 54, right and basically look like you had no medical problems according to the forms you filled except being a 1 1/2 pack a day smoker and occasionally taking some antacids. Let's examine you, Jerry. Why don't you take your shirt off please." I said.

As Jerry turned around, I saw lots of scars around his lateral right posterior region of his chest.

"Jerry, you never said you had any surgery on your chest. What's this from?" I asked.

"Those are stab wounds, Doc. Got 'em pretty bad when I was in a gang back in Chicago in my late teenage years." he replied.

Jerry continued, "I've lived a pretty rough life, Doc. Gangs as a teenager. Then I was in the Mob. I had to do some pretty bad things back then and I'm pretty ashamed of it. I had to do some time for it in my 20's. I probably did a lot of favors for taking care of this one bad egg though. After I got out, I was set up in Vegas and things went well. Made lots of money but something was missing. A life. Kind of lonely out there."

He continued, as he opened up his heart, "A wrong number changed my life. There she was on the other end of the line and she didn't hang up. We talked and talked and talked for over 2 hours and then we met in Oklahoma. We stayed in touch almost daily and then it happened. I asked her to marry me and we decided to start fresh back here."

"Amazing." I said in wonderment about his story. But I was also amazed at how open he was since I was a virtual stranger to him to tell his story to me.

"Now, Doc, I'm getting a lot of burning in my chest and stomach. Doc, let me tell you something. Now listen, you gotta be straight with. I'm a straight shooter. No BS now. Tell me if my heart is OK." Jerry said.

After I examined and took a history from Jerry, I responded, "I think the majority of your symptoms are excessive acid production causing irritation of your esophagus. This is what a record of the upper GI you had in Vegas a couple of years ago showed and the Zantac should help you but let's run an exercise cardiac stress test to determine if you have any cardiac problems which could also cause symptoms. You also need to quit smoking, Jerry." I said.

"Let Me tell you something, Doc. I walked away from some pretty bad habits, bad women and bad people. I found a wonderful lady. She saved my life, Doc. She's five months pregnant and I'm in my early fifties and we're going to have a baby. Doc, I want to be OK so I'm going to give up those damn things. Can't smoke around the baby." he said.

"Congratulations, Jerry." I said.

Jerry continued, "Got to have some Zantac renewed. Oh, I can't be without that Zantac, Doc. Do you think I worry too much?" he continued, "Hey, I'm Italian. I worry. You're a gumba too, Doc."

I returned, "Half Sicilian, half Irish."

"That's a helluva good mix. Let me tell you something, Doc. I had a rough life. Done some things I'm ashamed of. Now, thanks to my wife, I really have been saved and pray everyday to God for letting this happen." he said.

"The Lord helps those that help themselves, Jerry." I said.

"Too-shay!" he returned.

Jerry was quite concerned about his health. He was worried about having a coronary. After three stress tests 12 months apart, I convince him that he had gastric esophageal reflux, a condition of acid from the stomach chronically irritating the esophageal lining; this condition was relieved with medication. He constantly re-visited and constantly inquired if I thought he was perfectly healthy. His only problem after he quit smoking was his high anxiety. His wife was in her 30's and they were about to have their first child.

He emotionally told me of his religious rebirth and faith in God. He felt shame over his past and noted he had been involved with mob violence in his youth and had spent time in prison. He felt overjoyed that his life could be graced with a wonderful wife and child, living in a rural and private world apart from the urban jungles of his youth or the seamy underworld and money culture of Las Vegas.

He needed reassurance that it was okay not to be afraid any more, that life actually could be good to him, and that his life was not in danger.

Jerry returned after about his third visit.

"Well, Jerry, your stress test was fine. It is not an absolutely perfect test but you did so well on the treadmill I think you don't have to pursue this further right now. You have to stop smoking, Jerry." I said.

Jerry nodded in agreement and said, "I think I'll try the patch."

"Sounds good to me. You try whatever works, Jerry." I said and continued, "Hey, Jerry, after we talked about last time, have you ever thought of talking to kids with juvenile problems that have gotten in trouble. Maybe you could help them or inspire them somehow to see how you've changed."

Jerry looked up, "Doc, I'm ashamed of what I did. They need to look up to people more like you, Doc. People who have made something of their lives. I am working with the youth group through our church now and I really enjoy it.

"You have, too, Jerry. You've changed and now you're raising a family and gotten out of something bad. Jerry, sometimes those kids need a voice of experience, somebody who has been through the school of hard knocks." I said.

"I think about those kids often, Doc. They have no real home, sometimes no parents. The kids in the city are stuck in that urban jungle with no future. That was how I felt. I was lucky to get out alive. Most of them aren't." he said.

I thought about what Jerry said and flashed back to my residency days at a poor urban inner city hospital when gang violence brought the carnage in with gunshots and stab wounds into our Emergency Room. I wonder if any of them are still alive or if it changed their lives.

Jerry's life and transformation is a living and shining example that hope springs eternal. The day he brought in his newborn son revealed a man who had left a past unimaginable behind.

Whenever His Heart Desired

◆

Old John wandered in again. He never kept his scheduled appointment but seemed to show up at any time his heart desired. He was very unkempt, his clothes carrying a profuse odor.

John was standing near my exam room sink filling gallon jugs of water as I entered.

"What are you doing, John?" I asked.

"Water pump's busted, Doc. I had to get some water." he replied.

"Well, help yourself." I said and wondered how he was getting along and if he ever bathed.

"How are you getting along?" I asked.

"OK. I'm out of those blue pills. Ran out last week." John said.

John was taking medication for cardiac disorder, an enlarged prostate and diabetes. He never tested his sugar and he ate as he pleased. We tested him for his blood sugar frequently. He would not let the Public Health Nurse in his domain which was this little shack out in the country to test him.

I went to my PDR to check which color medicine translated the one he was out of. Well, his blood sugar and prostate meds were ok. When I looked, it was his beta blocker.

On examination, I noticed that his heart rate was very rapid, and I asked him, "John, are you dizzy, short of breath, or had any chest pain recently?"

"No, not that I can recall at the time," he said.

"Your heart's going at 150 beats a minute and you are not a little short of breath when you walk?" I asked.

"Well, I don't know. I don't walk fast enough to know." he said.

"Why aren't you taking those pills?" I asked.

"What pills. The little blue ones or those yellow ones or the white ones. What pills are you talking about?" he said confused.

"Do you look at the labels, John?" I asked.

"Can't read them." he continued, "The little blue pills, took the vitality out of me."

"Did they make you tired?" I asked.

"No, can't say they did." he answered.

"Then why did you stop them?" I asked.

"I told you why. Took my manhood away." he said.

John pulled out his bottles of medicine. It was obvious that he wasn't taking his beta blocker that was prescribed for him.

John was functionally illiterate, mildly hearing impaired, and had early stages of dementia. He was living alone and still driving, much to numerous attempts to get his license taken away. He was in a tachycardia, at a rate of about 150 beats per minute. He had taken a beta blocker to control his heart rate, and because he had mild angina, often exertion or stress triggered a rapid heart rate. Now, though, he was unsure if was taking the beta blocker. Then he perked up.

"Oh, those pills," he said, "No, they took all the vitality out of me."

I administered a beta blocker medicine in my office and after an hour's wait, he converted back into regular rhythm. While he was waiting on a cardiac monitor, I entered another room where an elderly woman was present. As I entered, she spoke up.

"Is that John So&So? God, he looks terrible and he really smells. You know, Doc, in his day he chased after more ladies in nearby towns than I can think of. They say he was pretty spry up to a pretty ripe old age. Pretty wild fellow. Always had a good time with the ladies." she said.

Stunned, I was having trouble imagining this man as a stud master of the past. It just wasn't registering seeing him in his present state.

Then it dawned on me that Old John stopped the beta blocker because it affected his sexual function. He was 80 years old and still spry, but his ticker needed this medicine.

I had to contact the Sheriff to make sure John had a driver's license. I couldn't imagine that he could have renewed his license in the past five years, but I knew he would present a safety hazard on these country roads.

John needed to go into a proprietary home, but he refused.

I asked myself how often men, like John, don't take the necessary medicines because of problems such as sexual dysfunction or other reasons that they won't tell their doctors about.

After John was kept in the office for a couple of hours after his beta-blocker was readministered his heart rate did come down to normal limits and he was feeling fine and was able to go home.

Well, we saved a potential $5,000 Medicare hospital stay that day. This happens every day, picking up on what seems like a minor problem can turn into an extended hospital stay at a high price tag.

This is the key to keeping medical cost down: timely prevention and intervention.

Well Old John always seemed to add an interesting dimension to a diverse practice. He will be missed when his untimely visits no longer come. Hopefully, if he continues taking his medication, he will be around a little longer.

Old John, despite needing some hygiene adjustments, was truly a happy old soul. He enjoyed his hermit life. Empowered by the freedom to live as he chose, he had very few wants or needs. This character could not easily be convinced to change. As his medical condition required me to have his driver's license canceled, he surprisingly adapted, maintained his little shack in the country, and—with the help of some nearby neighbors and relatives—he continued to do as his heart desired.

Shotgunning It

◆

As a strong believer in physical fitness, I prepared for my noon-hour jog on a hot summer day. My run would take me out of my office, up Pine Hill through an evergreen forest, and then out onto paths through farmers' fields and back through the grounds of our local school's athletic fields.

My staff was concerned as of recent and warned me to watch out for "'coons." For the past year, an epidemic of rabies had hit the raccoon population. Raccoons are usually nocturnal creatures but when stricken with rabies, they were often coming out in the daylight hours and acting peculiar. I would get as many as ten calls a week about a 'coon that had tangled with someone's dog. The 'coon most likely was rabid, and if saliva from the rabid 'coon reached the pet and a human with an open wound then touched the pet, rabies could be transferred. This circumstance led to a near panic among townspeople and an expensive endeavor to give immune globulin and vaccination for those at risk of demanding it—at a cost of $1,500 per person

Well, I never saw a raccoon on my runs all summer. But after my long run, as I was prepared to shower in my office's basement shower, I looked up, and there at my cellar window, which was wide open, was a very sickly, rabid raccoon. It was attempting to get into the room with me.

Startled, I quickly closed the window with heart pounding, and I ran upstairs half dressed in running gear to inform my staff.

One of my nurses, a gun enthusiast, left and quickly returned with her pistol in hand. Then a neighbor joined in. What a sight this was! My nurse and my neighbor, surrounding my office during regular hours, and armed to the hilt!

I went back down to my shower. As I looked up from my shower, which has a window above it, I was stunned to be looking directly down the barrel of a rather large shotgun. I was glad I had in fact finished my duties in the shower room!

After dressing, I went back outside. The critter had crossed the parking lot. My neighbor chased up Pine Hill, gun in hand. Bang! Mr. rabid raccoon was no longer. It was too bad that it had to happen, but he was obviously rabid, and dispatching him on the spot was one way to handle the situation.

When in doubt, shotgun it. I thought how often that is true in the way we practice medicine, especially in an urgent situation or with a demanding patient. You shoot out all sorts of diagnostic tests to protect yourself from and questions of any possible future litigation.

I used caution while running, but I never expected to see a rabid raccoon trying to join me for a shower. My guard was down.

Sometimes, any day in medical practice, one's guard could be down. When one least expects it, something may happen to a patient, or someone may want to sue. Often, insurance companies add an interesting twist and deny diagnostic or therapeutic procedures. Then enter the lawyers, who salivate at the thought of instant riches with one-third of awards going their way.

As I dozed off that night I thought of all the events of the day. In my dream state, I was served notice of a lawsuit at the office. With the delivery of the message, my palms became sweaty and my forehead was beginning to perspire. A queasy feeling came upon me in my stomach as the deliverer was serving me the papers. Suddenly, the deliverer of the papers looked very funny and blurry and the next thing I know he was foaming at the mouth. He tried to bite me. He started chasing me around the office. The next thing I know my Nurse got her gun out and scared him away. She was my hero.

I awoke, shaking my head and getting a glass of juice. It was time to go to work. Laughing on my drive to the office that morning, it occurred to me that somehow now we will eventually overcome this rabies epidemic and be able to live in an environment free of this dreaded disease. So true and how true it was that hopefully someday we could exist free from fear of excessive litigation driven by those infected with pure greed.

We have overcome a rabies epidemic. Certainly we can enact malpractice reform. Everyone will benefit. Well, almost everyone—with the exception of those infected with greed.

A bee-liever

◆

A BRIEF INTRLUDE IN the early afternoon prompted me to reach for Dr. Andrew Wiel's book , Spontaneous Healing. It had grabbed my curiosity. New horizons of possibilities to alternative approaches in medical treatment was a subject that I knew I had to investigate.

It seemed as if every day someone would approach me about an unconventional form of medical therapy that I was often clueless about.

A chart was thrown down in front of me . It was a nonverbal from my nurse to get back in the real world and get to work. Time to see Helen.

"A sweltering August afternoon reminded me how nice AC can be. Opening the door to Room 5, I peeked in and there was Helen, a prim and proper lady of 80 sitting in the chair against the wall look up with her head bobbing around and around. She kind of reminded me of those little plastic football models with bobbing heads you used to see in the back of cars when I was a kid. "What's wrong, Helen?" I asked.

"My neck is hurtin' and I'm gettin' dizzy since I've been in this room, Doc." she replied.

"Why are you looking up and bobbing your head?" I asked, "And how long have you been doing that?"

"Just since I got in this room. I've been watching those bees around your light, it seems to be getting more and more of them." she replied.

I looked up to see about 10 bees buzzing around above both of us around the light.

"Helen, let's move to a different room." I said.

I called for some help to get some bee spray and get Helen out but Helen was moving slow. My nurse knew a fellow, a professional bee keeper who could come right over and check out the problem. While she summoned Wes on the telephone I returned to fetch Helen out of the room. When I entered the room there were probably 100 bees swarming around us.

"Come on, Helen, we've got to move." I said and quickly hurried her out of the exam room and shut the door soundly behind us.

"Helen, let's get you in Room 2 and I'll be right back." I said.

"Doc." Helen said.

"Yeah." I replied.

"I think I got stung by a few bees in there." Helen said.

"Are you allergic to bees?" I asked.

"No, I don't think so, Doc." she replied. "I'll be OK."

"Let's get some ice on it and I'll be right back, OK." I said.

"OK, Doc. Take your time. I'm in no hurry today. Kind of nice to be out of the house. My husband drives me crazy some days anyways. Maybe that's why my neck hurts and maybe it's just that damn rheumatoid arthritis." she chuckled.

Soon Wes, the beekeeper, arrived to assess the situation.

"Borrow your stethoscope, Doc?" Wes asked.

"Sure, why not." I said.

Wes went to work like a skilled surgeon. He fearlessly entered Room 5 with now hundreds of bees swarming around him while we all waited outside behind the closed door "anxiously awaiting his diagnosis and prognosis".

Wes reappeared. "Doc, I've located the hive in the corner under the floorboards. This is a nice stethoscope, Litman, huh." he said.

"Yes, a Litman." I replied.

"Well, we'll have to operate, Doc. I'll be right back." Wes said.

Wes reappeared a few minutes later from his car with a power saw, chisel, hammer and nails and went to work fearlessly. In no time he found and disposed of the hive.

"Painters must have sealed the bees outside exit from the building" he said, "and they found a better route along your baseboard heating pipes. All in all the operation was a complete success, Doc. That will be $75.00."

"Do you take Blue Cross/Blue Shield?" I said.

"No, just cash, Doc." he chuckled.

"Well, thanks a lot Wes for coming over so soon." I said.

With all the excitement over and, in the meantime, seeing four other patients during the time Wes was working, I forgot all about poor Helen in Room 2.

"Helen, I'm sorry I kept you waiting. Now about your neck?" I asked.

"Well, Doc, something funny happened after I got stung and used a little ice and sat here about a half hour, my neck pain went away. So I guess I don't need to take up anymore of your time, Doc. Doc, I didn't know you were into alternative medicine treatment." she laughed.

"Me either, Helen. But what about your dizziness." I asked.

"Well, that was from staring at the bees so long with a sore neck, I'm better now. Listen Doc, you have a nice day and bee careful." she chuckled.

Well, Helen, Wes and the bees made my day. On that day, a conventional treatment for a neck disorder turned into a haphazard alternative treatment yielding a positive result all in rather a strange way. Strange is the way many conventional doctors look at alternative therapies. Many alternative methods and medical treatment have been with us for thousands of years but yet, much of conventional treatment today by physicians have tended to ignore the value alternative approaches offer in our time. Hopefully, we will begin to incorporate the treatment of herbal medicine, acupuncture and other remedies to help individuals overcome chronic disease and disorders. That strange twist of events that day began to make me a BEE-liever.

A Boaring Story of Courage

———————— ◆ ————————

Harold hobbled into the office quietly approaching the front desk window. Polite as he is always was, he proceeded to inform my receptionist, "Had a little accident with one of my boars. I stop the bleeding so I can wait if Doc's got time to look at." Harold said calmly.

"Harold, let me put you in the treatment room and clean up that wound." My Nurse replied.

"Oh, that's OK. All of these other people are scheduled ahead of me especially that mother with her child who looks a little sick ought to go ahead of me. I'll be fine." Harold said, "I'll just grab a Field & Stream."

A half hour had passed and Harold was next to be seen.

"Hi, Harold. What's going on?" I asked.

"One of my boars got the better of my leg, Doc. Got a pressure dressing on it and cleaned it with some peroxide."

Removing the dressing, an 6-inch long gash in his upper left thigh came very close to vital areas. But luckily for him would require cleaning, debridement and simple closure.

"How did this happen, again, Harold?" I asked.

"I was boared." he grinned.

"Helluva solution for 'boredom'." I joked back.

"Those horns can be sharp, Doc. This stubborn one gave me a hard time today." Harold chuckled.

"How do you have time to raise pigs with the kind of hours you're putting in at your job at the brewery?" I asked.

"Well, once a farmer, always a farmer." he said and winked a little as the Lidocaine anesthetized his thigh. He continued, "Got 1 year til I retire and then I'll be back farming and raising hogs and heifers for a hobby."

"Great." I said.

After finishing a closure he was satisfied with it and cleaning the wound, again I palpated a lymph node larger than normal in his left groin.

"Howard, have you ever noticed this?" I asked.

"Oh, I was going to mention that to you, Doc. It seems about a month ago I noticed it, but I thought it would go away." he said.

"Have you felt OK, lately?" I asked.

"Felt like I had a little virus for a few weeks, a little tired." he replied.

Palpating his abdomen, a discrete mass was palpated in his mid-left abdomen.

"Harold, I think I'd like you to have this lymph node biopsied and have a Cat Scan of your belly." I said.

"Problem, Doc?" he asked with somewhat alarmed eyes.

"Better safe than sorry, Harold." I said, "I'll see you back the day after your tests are completed and also when your stitches are ready to come out."

"OK, Doc." Harold replied.

The next morning Harold's Cat Scan showed a tumor in his abdomen behind his intestine. The following day a biopsy of the lymph node by a surgeon showed Non-Hodgkins lymphoma. Harold returned, already aware that somehow his life had just turned upside down.

"Doc, give it to me straight. I know you will." Harold said.

"Harold, the Cat Scan showed a tumor and the biopsy of the lymph node in your groin showed a type of lymphoma which is a cancer of the lymph glands. It is also, most likely, the same lymphatic cancer going on in your abdomen. You're going to need to see a cancer specialist as soon as possible and probably need more diagnostic tests to determine the extent of the disease." I said.

"Can I bring my wife in?" he asked.

"Of course." I said. "I'm sorry, I didn't know Mary was with you."

Mary entered quietly and the same story was carefully unloaded on this couple who had been married for 35 years and knew what the mutual age of 55, that their lives and their family's had forever changed with this knowledge.

"Doc, can it be cured?" Mary asked.

"Mary, we have to get Harold to an oncologist to stage the disease or to determine how far advanced it is. Then we will know the answers. I will send you to a specialist who is extremely knowledgeable but also has a great way with people going through this problem" I said.

"Thanks, Doc. That means a lot to us." Harold said.

Two and a half years passed. Harold stopped in for a routine visit.

"Haven't seen you in awhile, Harold, but I've been reading about you in your Specialist's report." I said. "It's been about 8 months since you've been in."

"Can't quite get into remission, Doc. Been on chemo and Prednisone for nearly two years now. It is beginning to wear me down. But I'm retired now and want to lick this damn disease."

I thought of all the toxic drugs and steroids pumped into his system. Was it all that modern medicine had to offer to him I asked myself ? It seemed to me with the explosion of technology and information worldwide that in the late 1990's we could do better. His bone marrow and liver were so weakened from the chemo. His bones were thinning to the danger of pathologic fractures of the spine from Prednisone, that I started him on medicine for his osteoporosis and for his bone thinning with medication to stabilize his bones. I suggested he take a substance called Milk Thistle and some antioxidant vitamins and selenium because European and Oriental studies as searched on the Worldwide Web showed benefits to the bodies of those undergoing chemotherapy. In the right doses, these substances would not harm him and they also had the benefit of giving Harold some empowerment over his immune system.

"Doc, I appreciate your time and I do feel a little better since I've been taking the supplements." Harold said after returning six weeks later.

Harold continues to live an active life. He refuses to lay down and resign. "Got too much living to do." he said and winked as he gracefully strolled out of the room and out into his life. He was in no way bored with his life.

The Gift

———————— ◆ ————————

It is the force that heals and creates. It is possessed by artists, athletes, teachers, and scientists.

It allows us to face adversity every day. It helped that farmer and corporate worker to overcome occupational stress. It guided that young pregnant teenage mother to chart her future. It was crucial to those folks addicted to alcohol, nicotine, and cocaine and to those with eating disorders to overcome their problems. It allowed those loving caretakers, whose spouses had deteriorated with Alzheimer's disease or other physical disorder, to persevere. It provided hope and acceptance to those facing cancer treatment. It allowed extended families to cope with the effects and consequences of divorce and family breakup upon young children. It is needed to overcome physical and learning disabilities and the darkness of depression.

In all these stories, there may be a common thread of relevance that touches upon your individual life.

The gift has the power to heal many problems and provides the strength to face enormous odds in many afflictions.

Physicians can help set this gift into motion in each individual by conveying a positive message of honest hope, alleviating fears, and connecting with the individual. They are in essence the modern-day shamans. The signals they convey, verbal and non verbal, often are instrumental in a person's attitude and long-term view of their own health.

But beyond the influence of physicians, the most important factor is unlocking and opening the gift. It lies within all of us but many never receive it. It may be realized for brief periods by some, but everyday stressors and time commitments tend to conceal it.

It can be seen in the eyes of our children.

It is living in the present with an unconditional love of life itself.

And in this state of being, the gift of inspiration springs forth.

Inspiration touches life from within and enacts change. Inspiration touches others' lives and offers hope. It is the force required in all our lives to overcome adversity, disease, and despair. Living in this state brings health and positive changes to all willing to unlock its enormous potential.

This gift has always been with us and will remain. Opening it up for all to see will overcome obstacles modern medicine faces and eventually transform the world to create a better society for each coming generation.

Printed in the United States
4192